COMP VALANCE

VALANCE

The TIME-TRAVELLING SANDWICH BITES BACK

By
MATT
BROWN

Illustrated by
LIZZIE FINLAY

D0390886

USBORNE

Introducing Compton Valance, his friends and family...

COMPTON VALANCE*

BRYAN NYLON
Compton's best friend ever.
(He really likes custard.)

* I know what you're thinking. "Compton Valance" isn't a real name. It's one of those made-up names that sounds a bit funny. Like "Nugget McDoo" or "Basil Burger". But, actually, it is a real name, and it's the name of our main character. And I'm going to tell you why. Well, I'm not, because that would take up a whole extra book. But I am going to tell you how to say it. So after three, say with me... One, two, three:
COM-TON VAAL-AAN-SE – You've got it!

First published in the UK in 2014 by Usborne Publishing Ltd., Usborne House, 83-85 Saffron Hill, London EC1N 8RT, England. www.usborne.com

Text copyright © Matt Brown, 2014
Illustrations by Lizzie Finlay © Usborne Publishing Ltd., 2014

The right of Matt Brown to be identified as the author of this work has been asserted by him in accordance with the Copyright, Designs and Patents Act, 1988.

Design: Hannah Cobley, Brenda Cole,
Neil Francis, Sarah Cronin and Katharine Millichope.
Editorial: Rebecca Hill and Becky Walker.

The name Usborne and the devices ♀ ⊕ are Trade Marks of Usborne Publishing Ltd.

A CIP catalogue record for this book is available from the British Library.

FMAMJJASON D/16

ISBN 9781409567783 04065-1

Printed in India

Chapter 1

How Compton Valance Became THE MOST POWERFUL BOY IN THE UNIVERSE

1. One day, one very ordinary boy took one very ordinary cheese-and-pickled-egg sandwich to school for his packed lunch.

2. But Compton FORGOT about the ordinary cheese-and-pickled-egg sandwich in his lunchbox and let it go all **mouldy** and **oldy** and **stinky** at the bottom of his school bag for three weeks.

3. Then, when the **stink** stunk so **stinkily** that Compton thought his hooter might shrivel up in shock, he and his best friend Bryan Nylon decided to **conduct an experiment** and place the sandwich in a shoebox at the back of Compton's wardrobe for another ten weeks. *

DO NOT OPEN FOR TEN WEEKS

(When you see a * you usually need to look at the bottom of the page. Go ahead, look below!)

* The sandwich was so stinky that, when handling it, Compton and Bryan had to wear the fail-safe protective clothing of dressing gowns on backwards, gardening gloves and swimming goggles!

4. After the sandwich had **sweated** and **stenched** for ten weeks, Compton and Bryan took it out of the shoebox. The sandwich was now a disgustingly **HIDEOUS** green colour, and on closer inspection it looked both **slimy** and a bit cat-sicky, while the inside was all browny, **sludgy** and **gooey**. Yum.

The **whiff** was also so bad that it smelled like a herd of rhinos **FARTING** in Compton and Bryan's faces.

5. In the name of science, Compton and Bryan popped a small piece of the **disgusting** sandwich in their mouths and **swallowed.**

And, to their surprise, they discovered that their mouldy, oldy sandwich had turned into a fizzing, whizzing **TIME MACHINE...**

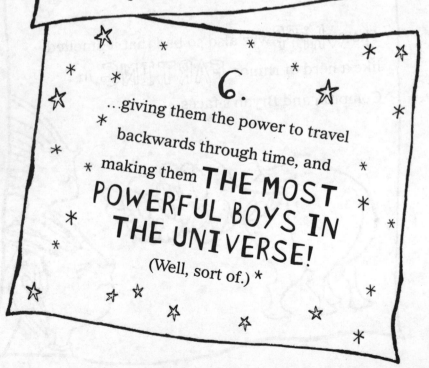

6.

...giving them the power to travel backwards through time, and making them **THE MOST POWERFUL BOYS IN THE UNIVERSE!**

(Well, sort of.)

*A WARNING ABOUT MAKING **TIME MACHINE SANDWICHES!** It is vitally important to use very strong English cheddar and a home-made pickled egg in order to attain full **TIME-TRAVEL-SANDWICH** capabilities. In 2034 a French scientist called Henri Tromper attempted to create a **TIME MACHINE SANDWICH** using Brie, raw onions and pickled frogs' legs. The results were so **CATASTROPHIC** that Tromper and his laboratory were immediately shut down and Tromper and two other scientists were confined to the toilet for the next eighteen years.**

****ANOTHER WARNING!** Actually, it's probably best you don't try any of this at home. Only attempt to create a **TIME MACHINE** within the appropriate **TIMEVAC 3000** Mobile Laboratory.

Chapter 2

An Embarrassing Incident Involving Baked Beans and a Very Important Person Indeed

Becoming **THE MOST POWERFUL BOY IN THE UNIVERSE** wasn't quite as much fun as **COMPTON VALANCE** had imagined.

The one MASSIVE drawback
with the whole time-machine experience
seemed to be that no sooner did you
acquire the ability to travel backwards
and forwards through time,

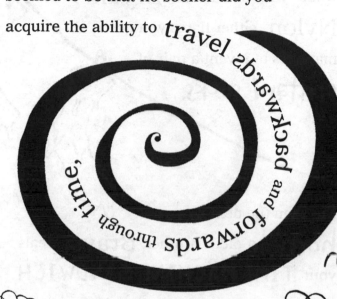

than it was cruelly snatched away from you.
One day you're BURPING

your way through history, accidentally
wiping out the dinosaurs
using a packet of custard creams,

turning your dad into a **woman**, and creating a PARALLEL UNIVERSE where your best friend, **Bryan Nylon**, either hates you or manages to invent a pair of custard socks...

But then the next day, your **horrible** older brother, **Bravo**, steals your **TIME MACHINE SANDWICH**, turning you back into just another ten-year-old boy standing in a room with your best friend and a man in a **tight** silver suit from the *twenty-seventh century.* *

(Look across for this one!)

12

"I can't believe it's GONE," said Compton sadly. "We only had the **TIME MACHINE SANDWICH** for a day. One. Lousy. **Stinking.** *Day!*"

He sat down heavily on his bed.

"Until about five minutes ago, today was going to be the BEST tenth birthday in the whole history of the world," Compton said, with a weary <sigh.>

"Now, though, it's turning into the **worst** ever day, EVER."

* This man is SAMUEL NATHANIEL DANIELS, a government agent from the future whose job it was to destroy the sandwich before it got into the wrong hands (Bravo's). He didn't get the job done. Bravo got the sandwich.

"What?" said Bryan. "Even worse than that time when your dad woke you up while you were standing in the kitchen weeing into your school bag because you'd dreamed it was a toilet?"

Compton gave Bryan a steely glare. He did not like being reminded of that terrible evening, or "The Night Of A Thousand Wees" as it had quickly become known within the Valance family.

After finding out about Compton weeing in his school bag, it had taken Compton's brother, Bravo, precisely thirty seconds to come up with the nickname Compton Wee Wee.

Ten minutes later that nickname became Compwee Wee Wee. Then Wee Wec Wee Wee, which was soon shortened to Wee Wee, then Wee Bum, Bum Bum, Bum Face, Bum Face Wee Wee, and finally Doctor Piddlepants.

Compton shuddered at the memory.

"How could we have been so STUPID?" he said, changing the subject back to the stolen TIME MACHINE SANDWICH.

"I know," said Bryan, taking a piece of paper out of his pocket and thrusting it under Compton's nose. "I'd written out this whole list of things we were going to do when we travelled back in time and we *only* managed to do the first one."*

* The things on Bryan's to do list were:

1. Go back to the time of the dinosaurs
2. Capture a sabre-toothed tiger and keep it as a pet (if can't find a sabre-toothed tiger, a woolly mammoth will do)

3. Go back to last week so I can take spelling test again and get the answers all right for once

4. Take a worm and a calculator back to the beginning of time and leave them in a box (see if I can create a new breed of superworm)

5. Go back three days to chess club and NOT call Mrs Zemekis "Mummy"

Outside Compton's bedroom window, it was raining over **Little Hadron** and the entire sky was dark grey. It perfectly matched Compton and Bryan's mood.

As the boys sat glumly on Compton's bed, Samuel Nathaniel Daniels paced nervously round the room, looking at his **W.A.T.CH.** (That's a **W**rist **A**ctivated **T**ime **CH**anger, invented in <u>**2589**</u> to allow the wearer to travel forwards or backwards in time to any point or place.)

THE COMMISSIONER's not going to like this,

he said.

"Who's 'The Commissioner'?" asked Bryan.

"Who's THE COMMISSIONER? Er, only the most **HUGELY important person** in the whole of the **FPU***." Samuel Nathaniel Daniels sighed. <sigh.>

* **FPU** stands for **Future Perfect Unit**, which is the twenty-seventh century government time-travel department that Samuel Nathaniel Daniels works for.

It was all supposed to be so **simple,**

he said. "All I had to do was come **back** to the twenty-first century, set up a **top secret** observation unit in the house over the road to monitor your activity, wait until you used the **TIME MACHINE SANDWICH**, come over and introduce myself, **grab** the **sandwich**, travel forward in time by **650 years**, fill out form 1999, take the form to Len in **Disposal**, **quarantine** the **sandwich**, fill out form 1895 in duplicate and make sure to send one to Wendy over in **Sector ZX81**, retrieve the **sandwich** from **quarantine**, isolate the **sandwich** in **Perma-Ice**, put it in a **Hypa-Crate**, put the **Hypa-Crate** onto a **MARSeeker** and then sit back

19

while the MARSeeker travelled the

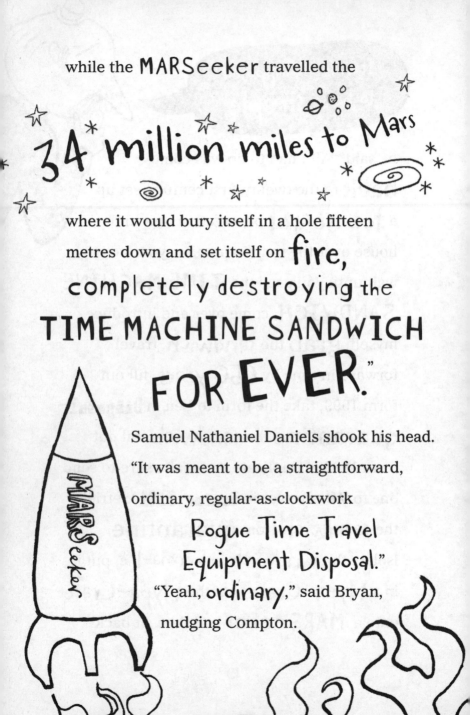

34 million miles to Mars

where it would bury itself in a hole fifteen

metres down and set itself on fire,

completely destroying the

TIME MACHINE SANDWICH

FOR EVER."

Samuel Nathaniel Daniels shook his head.

"It was meant to be a straightforward,

ordinary, regular-as-clockwork

Rogue Time Travel
Equipment Disposal."

"Yeah, ordinary," said Bryan,

nudging Compton.

"But now, thanks to your brother,"
Samuel Nathaniel Daniels went on,
"I am in trouble DEEPER than a
DEEP well that's SO DEEP
it has to have a sign saying

REALLY
DEEP WELL

put up next to it."

"Oh, boo-hoo to you," said Compton, suddenly rising to his feet and pointing at himself and Bryan. "We created a TIME MACHINE! On our own. We were all set to do some unbelievably COOL stuff this weekend. In fact, right now we were supposed to be engaged in a MASSIVE battle with Blackbeard the pirate so that we could find out where all his treasure was and make him walk the plank."

"OF COURSE!" yelled Bryan, grabbing a pencil and writing on the piece of paper in his hand.

"Blackbeard! I knew there was something I had forgotten to put on the list."

"And now," continued Compton, "my stupid, horrible brother Bravo has our TIME MACHINE SANDWICH that we invented, that we've had for just one single day, and is probably, as we speak, travelling through time and going anywhere his imagination takes him, having all the fun we should be having."*

* Luckily for Compton, Bravo's imagination was unbelievably small. In fact, some historians think that it might not have existed at all.

"What are we going to do?" asked Bryan, folding his list back up and putting it in his pocket.

Compton turned and looked out of his window at the drizzle beyond. "We're going to get our sandwich back," he said. "All I need to do is work out how."

Samuel Nathaniel Daniels was not taking recent events at all well. He slumped in the corner of the room, wrapped his arms around his knees and rocked himself gently from side to side.

Oh, I do hope The Commissioner has forgotten about the baked bean incident,

he said.

"*Baked bean incident?*" said Bryan. "What *baked bean incident?*"

"Well, let's just say that last year I accidentally dressed The Commissioner up like a baby and then accidentally managed to accidentally push her into a swimming pool FULL of baked beans, accidentally," said Samuel Nathaniel Daniels.

"**What?**" said Bryan. "How did *that* happen?"

Samuel Nathaniel Daniels's **W.A.T.CH.** began to buzz

"It's far too complicated to go into now," he replied, getting to his feet and looking nervously at the display. "Oh dear, it's The Commissioner. She wants me back in the twenty-seventh century immediately for a full debrief at the **FPU** headquarters."

The **W.A.T.CH.** buzzed again.

"That's not all," he added. "She wants to see **you two** as well."

Compton and Bryan looked at each other while Samuel Nathaniel Daniels fiddled with the settings on his **W.A.T.CH.** One second later the air in Compton's bedroom **crackled** and **fizzed** and they all **DISAPPEARED.**

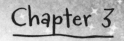

Chapter 3

The Theodore Logan Memorial Hall and Reception Zone at the FPU HQ

When the air around them stopped **crackling** and **fizzing**, Compton and Bryan looked about at their new surroundings. They were standing in one corner of an enormous, cavernous, domed room.

"Where are we?" said Compton, feeling just a little bit small.

"Well," said Samuel Nathaniel Daniels. "Right now we are in the

Theodore Logan Memorial Hall and Reception Zone

at the headquarters of the **Future Perfect Unit**."

A group of school children filed in and stood in the middle of the reception hall. "It's MASSIVE," said Bryan, looking around.

"And when are we exactly?" asked Compton. Samuel Nathaniel Daniels looked at his **W.A.T.CH.**

"Well, it's nine thirty in the morning of Saturday, twenty-third of April, 2664," he said. "Welcome to the twenty-seventh century."

A smile spread over Compton and Bryan's faces.

"We're in the FUTURE," said Compton.

"It's awesome! And just like I imagined," said Bryan. "All SHINY and bleepy."

A small shiny thing WHIZZED past bleeping.

"Right then, while you two get your bearings, I'll check in at the front desk and let them know we're here," said Samuel Nathaniel Daniels, striding across the hall. "Why don't you listen in on that school trip that's just about to start?" he called back. "You might learn something."

"WELCOME TO THE HEADQUARTERS OF THE Future Perfect Unit, TODAY WILL BE A DAY YOU WILL NEVER FORGET. TODAY YOU WILL GET TO SEE A LITTLE OF THE WORK THAT WE DO HERE AT THE FPU. WORK THAT HELPS MAKE ALL OUR LIVES SAFER."

Compton and Bryan stared at the strange contraption booming at them in a loud, mechanical voice as they wandered over to join the back of the school party.

"The future's a bit weird," said Compton to Bryan, who nodded.

"*Look*," whispered Bryan. "*That woman looks just like Samuel Nathaniel Daniels.*"

Sure enough, the school party had been joined by a woman wearing a tight silver suit and a bowler hat on her head.

"Hello, everyone," smiled the woman. "My name is Agent Hendrix and I'd like to welcome all of you this morning to the nerve centre of operations here at the **FPU**. "

As she spoke she pressed a button on her **W.A.T.CH.** and six doors suddenly appeared next to her.

ANIMAL TRAINING DIVISION [CUTE]

ANIMAL TRAINING DIVISION [SCARY]

LASERS, PHASERS & BLASTERS

Compton nudged Bryan. "Did you see

that?" he gasped.

"Now," Agent Hendrix continued, "behind

each of these doors in front of you are some

extraordinary new technologies that the

Future Perfect Unit is working on to help

in the battle against ILLEGAL TIME

TRAVEL. The question is, *which* door

would you like to go through first?"

A small blue screen flickered

into life on each door.

INVISIBILITY RESEARCH CENTRE

TIME TRAVEL VEHICLES [HOVER CARS, JET BIKES & ROCKET BALLS]

TIME CRIME DIVISION [RECORDS OF ALL ILLEGAL ATTEMPTS]

A great noise buzzed around the hall as the class discussed amongst themselves which of the many wonders they wanted to see first.

Er, excuse me?

said a small boy at the back.

The room fell silent once more.

"Yes?" said Agent Hendrix.

Er, can we go through **this** door too?

said the boy, pointing to an unremarkable door in the wall that no one else had seen.

COMPLETELY
ORDINARY
BROOM
CUPBOARD

"NO, I'm afraid not. It's just a **completely ordinary broom cupboard** where nothing of any interest happens," said Agent Hendrix.

> It is definitely NOT a hush-hush top secret operations room,

she added a little nervously. And with that, she ushered the children quickly through the first door –

ANIMAL TRAINING DIVISION [CUTE]

– and their tour began.

Samuel Nathaniel Daniels walked over to where Compton and Bryan were left standing.

"Come on," he said. "The Commissioner is expecting us. We've got to go."

"Where?" said Compton.

"In *there,*" said Samuel Nathaniel Daniels, pointing to the small door with the words:

COMPLETELY ORDINARY BROOM CUPBOARD

written on it.

Chapter 4

The Completely Ordinary Broom Cupboard

Samuel Nathaniel Daniels opened the door marked COMPLETELY ORDINARY BROOM CUPBOARD and he, Compton and Bryan all walked through. Inside was a small, cramped, dark room full of brooms. "It's a completely ordinary broom cupboard," said Compton.

A wicked smile flashed across Samuel Nathaniel Daniels's face.

"*Is it?*" he said mysteriously and began to move the brooms to one side. "Remember, in here NOTHING is what it seems."

Compton and Bryan watched and soon saw that behind the brooms was another door, this time marked:

TOTALLY NORMAL
MOP AND BUCKET
STORAGE
AREA

Samuel Nathaniel Daniels nodded towards the door.

Go ahead,

he said even more *mysteriously* than before.

Open it up and see what's inside.

Compton *nervously* pushed open the door marked TOTALLY NORMAL MOP AND BUCKET STORAGE AREA. Inside was a small storage area full of mops and buckets. Compton looked back at the others and sighed.

It's a **totally normal** mop and bucket storage area,

he said.

"Is it?" said Samuel Nathaniel Daniels, EVEN MORE mysteriously than the previously **even more** mysterious time.

Or is it something you would NEVER dream of in your **wildest** of wild imaginings?

With that, he moved aside all of
the mops and buckets to reveal
another door,
this time marked: ↰ RUN-OF-THE-MILL COMPARTMENT FOR TEA, COFFEE AND CHOCOLATE HIBNOBS

"Who among you DARES to step
across the threshold of reason?"
he said, turning to face the boys. "Remember
this moment, because NOTHING that
comes after it will

EVER be the SAME AGAIN."

Rolling his eyes, Compton pushed open
the door marked RUN-OF-THE-MILL
COMPARTMENT FOR TEA, COFFEE
AND CHOCOLATE HIBNOBS.*

* Chocolate Hibnobs are what people in
the twenty-seventh century called
CHOCOLATE HOBNOBS.

To his **amazement**, behind the door there **wasn't** *any* tea, coffee or biscuits to be seen. Instead, Compton found himself peering down a

gloomy corridor.

As he stepped into it, the corridor suddenly became **so** small and **cramped** that he and Bryan had to go through in single file and **duck down** when they walked, otherwise they would have hit their heads on the ceiling.

"Why is it so small?" asked Compton as he stoop-walked down the corridor.

"IT'S AN **ANTI-INTRUDER DEVICE**," shouted Samuel Nathaniel Daniels from the back of the line.

"What if the intruders are small **children?**" asked Bryan.

41

"Oh," said Samuel Nathaniel Daniels.

"We didn't think of *that*."

The three of them huffed and puffed and shuffled in a line down the dark, tight, miniature corridor,

turning this way and that as it

sssssssnaked

its way through the inside of the FPU building.

Eventually they came to a DEAD END.

WE'LL HAVE TO GO BACK,

shouted Compton over his shoulder
to the others.

WE CAN'T GO ANY FURTHER.

"Don't worry," said Samuel Nathaniel
Daniels from his position at the rear of the line.
"The wall in front of you is **actually** a
secret door. Just give it a tap."

Compton tapped the wall and, seemingly
from nowhere, a small drawer **whirred**
open.

"What do we do now?" called
back Compton.

"It's another anti-intruder device," said Samuel Nathaniel Daniels. "The drawer is like a lock, except we don't have a normal key. To open the door we use BRT, Bogey Recognition Technology."

"What on earth's *that?*" said Bryan.

"Oh, it's the *very latest* thing," said Samuel Nathaniel Daniels. "We've installed it on all the FPU's most secret doors. Basically, every human being has their own snot pattern.

It's completely unique to them and almost impossible to copy. You just need to put a bogey in the drawer and, hey presto, the door opens."

"Wow," said Compton. "So I just need to put one of my nose candies in to open it up?"

Not quite,

said Samuel Nathaniel Daniels, as he stuck one of his fingers up his nose and had a good rummage around.

Your snot pattern isn't in the system, so you'll have to put in one of my bogeys for it to work. I'll pass you one and you can pop it in.

What?

shouted Compton.

I'm not touching your snot!

"Me neither," said Bryan.

"Oh, come on, it's *just* a **bogey**," said Samuel Nathaniel Daniels. "And besides, you **have to,** otherwise we're stuck here."

Once Samuel Nathaniel Daniels had found a good, **juicy bogey,** he took hold of Bryan's hand and wiped it onto his middle finger.

Pass it on,

he instructed.

Scarcely able to believe the
HIDEOUS GROSSNESS

of what was happening, and with a look of horror etched onto his face, Bryan moved his hand v e r y s l o w l y round to where Compton was standing and wiped the nasal mucous onto Compton's hand.

Then, fighting the urge to be sick on the floor, Compton lowered his hand and wiped the schnozz slime into the drawer.

The drawer then whirred closed automatically and the corridor went silent.

Compton and Bryan wiped their hands furiously on their trousers.

After a few moments **three green lights** appeared on the wall in front of them and a door, which up until that *exact* second had been completely **invisible**, slowly **hiiissssed** open.

"Right," said Samuel Nathaniel Daniels. "Come on, let's go."

From the **cramped** conditions in the corridor, it took a moment for Compton and Bryan to quite believe what they saw beyond the **secret** door. They found themselves standing on a metal balcony, about twenty metres up the wall of the **BIGGEST ROOM** they had *EVER SEEN* in their lives.

In fact, this wasn't *just* a big room, it was a

colossally, GIGANTICALLY,

whompingly,

MASSIVELY,

ENORMO-
HUGELY BIG

ROOM.

It was so

ENORMO-HUGELY BIG

that Compton couldn't even see the other side
of the room and the ceiling was so high it felt
as though they were outdoors.

"AMAZING," gasped Bryan, as he
held tightly on to the railings in front
of him. "Look at *that*."

The walls of the room were brilliant white
and so BRIGHT that it took a few moments
for Compton's eyes to get used to the glare.

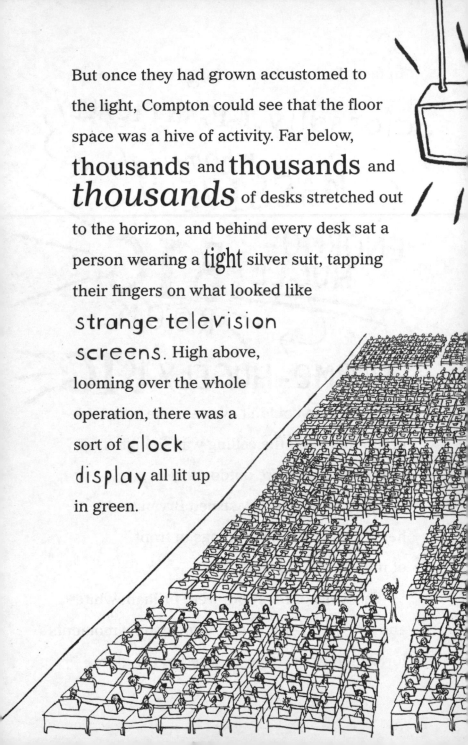

But once they had grown accustomed to the light, Compton could see that the floor space was a hive of activity. Far below, **thousands** and **thousands** and *thousands* of desks stretched out to the horizon, and behind every desk sat a person wearing a tight silver suit, tapping their fingers on what looked like strange television screens. High above, looming over the whole operation, there was a sort of clock display all lit up in green.

"I thought this was a *broom cupboard?*" said Compton.

"That's what we **want** people to think," said Samuel Nathaniel Daniels. "It's actually our

HUSH-HUSH TOP SECRET OPERATIONS ROOM.

Can you see the person over there in orange?"

Compton nodded. It wasn't hard to spot her when **every** other person in the room was wearing silver.

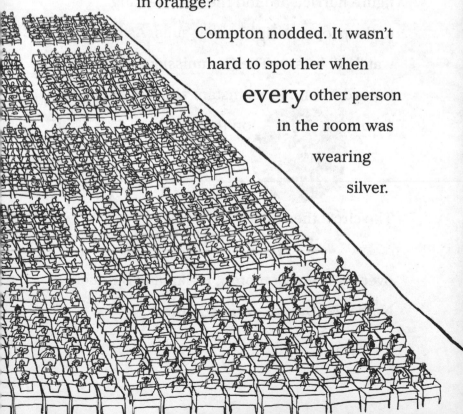

"That's THE COMMISSIONER," said Samuel Nathaniel Daniels.

"The one you shoved in a pool FULL of beans?" asked Bryan.

"Yes," said Samuel Nathaniel Daniels.

Compton watched as the small orange figure hurried around the floor, talking to the people in tight silver suits. As he watched, he saw The Commissioner look up towards them. In an instant she had hopped onto a BIG red circle on the floor.

The circle then rose up and floated over to where Compton, Bryan and Samuel Nathaniel Daniels were standing.

As The Commissioner came closer, Compton was able to fully absorb her most unusual look. She was dressed in a kind of furry, orange onesie. She wore shiny, tight gloves and a pair of see-through boots that looked like they were made of glass. But it was her body that Compton found most unusual of all. She had a l o n g, thin neck that must have been about four times longer than a normal person's, and perched on top of it sat her head, like a coconut on a fairground coconut shy. Dark, wavy hair cascaded down over her shoulders.

"*Agent Daniels,*" she snapped as she opened a small gate in the metal balcony railings and strode onto the runway like a supermodel crossed with a giraffe. "Is this who I think it is?"

"Y-yes, ma'am," said Samuel Nathaniel Daniels, very, very nervously. "May I present to your commissionership, Compton Valance and Bryan Nylon."

A smile immediately replaced the frown on The Commissioner's face and she grabbed Compton and Bryan's hands and shook them until they thought their wrists might *actually* come off.

"An absolute *delight* to see you two **at last,**" she said. "Simply **wonderful**. Been dying to meet you for ages."

The Commissioner turned and looked at Samuel Nathaniel Daniels. As she did, her smile was immediately replaced by yet another frown.

Agent Daniels,

she barked.

Go to the Drink Generator on Level Four and get some refreshments for our guests.

Yes, ma'am,

said Samuel Nathaniel Daniels.

"I will have instant tomato soup," commanded The Commissioner. "And there better **not** be any more *little accidents*."

"N-no, ma'am," said Samuel Nathaniel Daniels, his knees trembling slightly.

The Commissioner stared deeply into Samuel Nathaniel Daniels's eyes for what seemed like a very, v e r y, v e r y l o n g time.

"I'm watching you," she said finally. "No more accidents!"

"I think she still remembers **the beans**," whispered Compton to Bryan as Samuel Nathaniel Daniels sloped off to get the drinks.

Once he was gone, The Commissioner turned to Compton and Bryan and her smile returned once more.

Now then, where were we?

she said, thinking hard.

Ah, yes, thank goodness you two have arrived. We've got a MAJOR problem here, and we really, really need your help.

Chapter 5

How Having A Chat With Your Grandfather Can Lead To The DESTRUCTION OF THE UNIVERSE

The Commissioner motioned for both Compton and Bryan to join her aboard her flying red circle. As Compton stepped onto it, he felt the circle give a little under his weight and then spring back up once he was on board. It was what he imagined

stepping onto a **cloud** would feel like.

"Cool," Compton said to Bryan as he gently bounced up and down.

"No, it's *not*," muttered Bryan as his face turned the exact shade of green that his mum had painted their downstairs toilet.*

The Commissioner smiled, twiddled a silver disc that she held in the palm of her hand and the red circle began to descend slowly, sweeping over the desks below.

* Bryan Nylon was well known for being sick on all manner of transportation. He'd been car-sick, bus-sick, train-sick, plane-sick, taxi-sick, bike-sick, pogo-stick-sick and even on-top-of-his-dad's-shoulders-sick. So you can imagine how standing on a floating circle, six hundred years in the future was making him feel. **
** Sick!

59

"First things first," she said to Compton brightly. "HUGE congratulations on the sandwich, Colin."

"Er, my name's <u>Compton</u>," corrected Compton.

"Yes, I know," said The Commissioner. "Colin. That's what I said."

"Er, you said <u>Colin</u> again," said Compton.

"Yes!" said The Commissioner, smiling.

"But my name's <u>Compton</u>," repeated Compton.

The Commissioner's face fell.

"What did <u>I</u> say?" she said.

"<u>You</u> said <u>Colin</u>," said Compton.

"<u>Colin?</u>" said The Commissioner.

"<u>Colin</u>," nodded Compton in agreement.

The Commissioner forlornly shook her head.

"Then you have my deepest apologies, Colin," she said, ruffling his hair and adding, "I assure you it won't happen again."

Compton looked at Bryan and rolled his eyes.*

The Commissioner continued. "As I was saying, Colin, making your own TIME MACHINE really was extraordinarily clever. Do you know how long our most brilliant minds have been trying to work on an edible TIME MACHINE?"

* The Commissioner was widely regarded to be the cleverest person in the history of humanity. She had 438 degrees in subjects including Astrophysics, Marine Biology, Ancient History, Future History, Quantum Mechanics, Sword Fighting, Football Commentary, Balloon Modelling, Surfing, Criminology and Surfing Criminology. She was, however, really, really bad at remembering names.

Compton shook his head.

"Fifty-seven years, that's how long. And you two, YOU managed to perfect it in a few weeks. Quite, quite brilliant."

The Commissioner twiddled the disc again and the red circle swooped down to the ground and landed with a tiny bump.

"I would have put you up for a Medal of Commendation," she said as the three of them stepped off the circle. "And yet, you inventing the TIME MACHINE SANDWICH has rather left us in a bit of a fix, if you'll pardon the pun."

Compton looked at Bryan. "What's a pun?" he whispered.

"I dunno," said Bryan, shrugging his shoulders. "I think my mum gets them from the bakery."

The Commissioner strode across the floor of the **hush-hush top secret operations room**, checking the screens of the thousands and thousands and thousands of **FPU** agents as she went.

You see,

she continued,

we take security **VERY SERIOUSLY** here. The **FPU** has only ever lost TWO **TIME MACHINES** in the **WHOLE HISTORY OF ITS EXISTENCE**.

The first loss was relatively minor, although I'm afraid I CAN'T reveal any details as the **whole incident** is still completely and totally **TIP-TOP SECRET** until the year <u>3464</u>.*

* **THE FOLLOWING IS FOR READERS AFTER 3464 ONLY!** The first time machine that went missing was invented by Malcolm Coggins in the year 2551. Coggins's time machine was as small as a grain of rice but unfortunately also happened to look just like a grain of rice. After being accidentally eaten by Coggins's mother, it was eventually retrieved the next day after Mrs Coggins sat on a specially constructed toilet.

grain of rice

The incident subsequently led to the foundation in 2553 of the

FPU Sewage Department

(nicknamed the F-Pee-Ewww).

As they walked, Compton looked at the **FPU** agents sitting behind their strange screens. He noticed that above each screen was a number.

"Which leads us to the second lost time machine," continued The Commissioner. "Your cheese-and-pickled-egg sandwich."

The three of them stopped next to an **FPU** agent who had the number twenty-seven above her screen. Compton and Bryan watched the agent at work. There was NO keyboard to type on or mouse to click. Instead the agent seemed to just

Wave her hands

in front of the display to change things on it.

She was concentrating **so hard** on her strange screen that she didn't even notice the three new visitors next to her.

As I'm sure that **FOOL** Agent Daniels has explained,

said The Commissioner,

a time machine is a **DANGEROUS THING**, especially in the wrong hands. Going back in time and making even the slightest change to what **HAS** happened could have a **terrifying** impact on what **WILL** happen.

The **FPU** agent continued to input information into her screen.

For example, **imagine** if you travelled back in time fifty-seven years and asked a **stranger** for directions. Nothing **harmful** in that, is there?

Well, **no,** said Compton.

Sounds okay to me, added Bryan.

WRONG!

shouted The Commissioner, making Compton and Bryan "JUMP."

WRONG! WRONG! WRONG!

There is **everything** WRONG with that. You see, what I **didn't** tell you was that the stranger you asked directions from was **your grandfather**, who, on the very day that you travel back in time and meet him, was about to **bump into** a lady carrying a box of groceries home from the shops. **This lady** would become—

My grandma, interrupted Compton.

That's **how** my grandpa and grandma met each other. My dad told me all about it.

The Commissioner flashed a smile.

What **should** have happened,

she continued,

was that they **met**, fell in **love**, got **married**, and had your **father**, who **grew up**, **met** your mother, fell in **love**, got **married**, and had **YOU**. Right?

That's **right**, said Compton.

That's **exactly** what did happen.

WRONG!

shouted The Commissioner again.

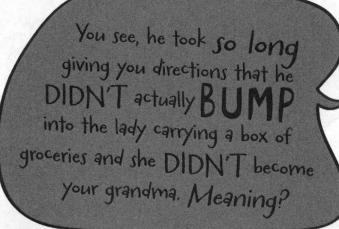

You see, he took so long giving you directions that he DIDN'T actually BUMP into the lady carrying a box of groceries and she DIDN'T become your grandma. Meaning?

Compton and Bryan looked blankly back at The Commissioner.

Meaning, she continued,

that your father was NEVER born, and if he wasn't born then YOU, Compton, were NOT BORN EITHER.

The impact of this **extraordinary** revelation took a moment to **sink in.**

Wow,

said Compton.

So you see, said The Commissioner,

that in the wrong hands, a time machine could cause some very, very BIG problems.

And Bravo is definitely the wrong hands,

said Compton*,

looking worriedly at Bryan.

* Historians have concluded that there was only **one person** who had a worse pair of hands than Bravo Valance, and her name was Susie Diamond. It is widely thought that if Susie had got hold of the sandwich she would have eaten it all in one huge mouthful, gone back to the beginning of time and squashed flat the new and very tiny universe, just by sitting on it.

The Commissioner started walking again past some more desks, until she reached another red circle on the floor. She stepped onto it and stopped. Compton and Bryan followed.

"What you see here," she said, "are all the *possible* futures that *could* happen now Bravo has the sandwich. Every single FPU agent has worked through one *potential* TIMELINE. Pick a number, any one you want."

"Er, ninety-seven," said Compton.

The Commissioner twiddled the silver disc in her hand and the red circle slowly lifted off the ground and swooped around the room until it came to a halt and hovered over the agent with the number ninety-seven above his screen.

"Ninety-seven is the **TIMELINE** where Bravo goes back in time and becomes a dandy highwayman who robs from the rich and then keeps all the loot for himself. In this particular **TIMELINE**, Bravo sets off a chain of events that leads to the **DESTRUCTION OF THE UNIVERSE** in just ten thousand years from now. Right, pick another number."

"Erm, 189,204," said Bryan.

The Commissioner twiddled the disc in her palm and once again the red circle was off flying around the room.

"Oh, now **this** is a good one," said The Commissioner, parking the red circle next to the agent with 189,204 above his screen. "In this *possible* future Bravo goes back to the court of Queen Victoria, where he blows his nose without a hanky and showers the Queen in snot.*

* Records show that she was NOT amused.

In the distance, Compton could see Samuel Nathaniel Daniels running and sweating over to where they were hovering.

HERE... WE... ARE... COMMISSIONER,

he shouted breathlessly up at the red circle just above his head. "I got you some instant tomato soup. Just as you like it."

The Commissioner eyed Samuel Nathaniel Daniels suspiciously.

"I hate blue cups," she said coldly. "Go away and fetch some more. And this time, *get it right!*"

She definitely remembers the baked beans,

whispered Bryan to Compton.

Samuel Nathaniel Daniels's shoulders drooped as he let out a **big sigh** and **jogged off into the distance.**

The Commissioner suddenly pointed to an agent near to where they had started.

OVER THERE, TIMELINE 232,

she **bellowed**.

Timeline 232
Bravo Valance attempts to become **EMPEROR OF THE UNIVERSE** and fails. Timeline ends with the **DESTRUCTION OF THE UNIVERSE in EIGHT HUNDRED YEARS.**

The Commissioner spun around quickly
and pointed at another agent.

TIMELINE 9321,

she screeched.

> **Timeline 9321**
> Bravo Valance actually *does* become
> **EMPEROR OF THE UNIVERSE.**
> **DESTRUCTION OF THE UNIVERSE in**
> **EIGHT YEARS.**

EIGHT YEARS!

shouted Compton.

But I'll only be
eighteen then.

It's alright for **you**,

said Bryan.

I'll only be **seventeen**.

OVER THERE,

yelled The Commissioner, completely ignoring Compton and Bryan's concerns.

Timeline 12
Bravo Valance loses the TIME MACHINE SANDWICH down the back of the sofa. DESTRUCTION OF THE UNIVERSE in **TWO HUNDRED AND FORTY-THREE YEARS.**

Suddenly she stopped, then wheeled round to face Compton and Bryan again.

Can you spot the **common theme** for all these TIMELINES?

she asked.

You shouting a lot,

said Bryan, wiggling his fingers in his ears. He was closest to The Commissioner and so had taken the brunt of her

EXTREMELY LOUD VOICE.

"The DESTRUCTION OF THE UNIVERSE?" said Compton.

"Precisely, Colin," said The Commissioner. "In fact, *every single* TIMELINE in this whole room ends with the DESTRUCTION OF THE UNIVERSE. Or rather, *every single* TIMELINE except for 112,358."

"What's different about *that* timeline?" asked Bryan.

"I'm glad you asked that," said The Commissioner, twiddling the silver disc in her hand. "Because what happens in that TIMELINE is very, very interesting."

And with that, the flying red circle swooped off in search of TIMELINE 112,358.

Chapter 6

Timeline 112,358

The agent sitting behind screen number **112,358** glanced up and saw The Commissioner heading his way. He licked his hand and tried to **flatten down** the wiry and rather **thick tangle** of hair that sat on his head like a dead badger. *

"Good morning, Agent Fibonacci," she said when she reached him.

---

* Or if not actually a DEAD badger, then certainly a very, very poorly one.

Agent Fibonacci smiled awkwardly and went **bright red.**

Agent Fibonacci,

The Commissioner continued,

has produced the **one TIMELINE** in the **WHOLE** of the operations room where Bravo **doesn't** trigger off a sequence of events that leads to the **DESTRUCTION OF THE UNIVERSE.**

"So **what** happens?" asked Compton eagerly as he and Bryan scanned the strange screen to try to see what kind of future this **TIMELINE** held.

Well you see, my dear, **dear boy,**

said The Commissioner, flashing a **brilliant** smile at him,

this is the timeline where you and Bryony and Agent Daniels **stop him.**

Wow, said Bryony, er, I mean, Bryan.

Awesome timeline. Way to go, Fibonacci!

Agent Fibonacci's face turned an *even redder* shade of red.

"So, you can see," said The Commissioner momentously, "that you two boys are the key to sorting this whole mess out."

Compton felt his mouth go VERY DRY.

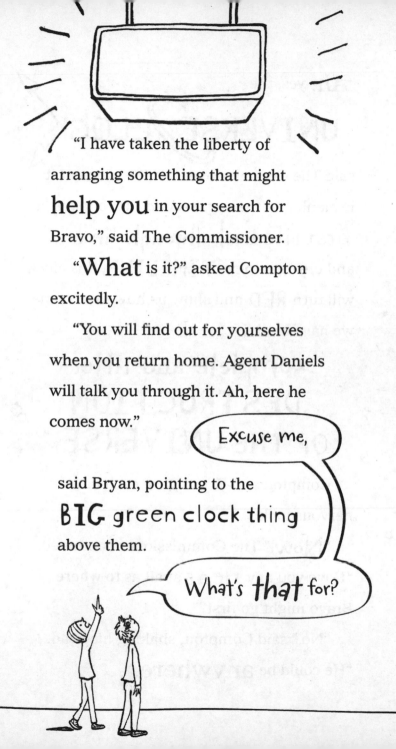

"I have taken the liberty of arranging something that might **help you** in your search for Bravo," said The Commissioner.

"**What** is it?" asked Compton excitedly.

"You will find out for yourselves when you return home. Agent Daniels will talk you through it. Ah, here he comes now."

Excuse me,

said Bryan, pointing to the **BIG** green clock thing above them.

What's **that** for?

"*Ah*, yes, the

UNIVERSE CLOCK ,"

said The Commissioner. "At the moment it is blank, but the *very second* Bravo takes his first bite back through time and creates a new TIMELINE, this clock will turn RED and show us how much time we have until the

complete and utter
DESTRUCTION
OF THE UNIVERSE ."

Compton and Bryan gave each other a nervous look.

"Now," The Commissioner continued. "Have you any ideas at all as to where Bravo might go first?"

"No," said Compton, shaking his head. "He could be anywhere."

"Any-when," Bryan added.

"In order to catch him," said The Commissioner, her eyes narrowing slightly, "you must put yourselves in his shoes. What would Bravo do with the power to travel back in time? Where would he go? You need to think like him; act like him; become him."

She placed a hand on Compton's shoulder and looked right into his eyes. "Remember, Colin.

The FATE of the ENTIRE UNIVERSE is in YOUR HANDS…"

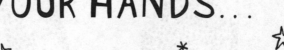

Chapter 7

Kill All Humans!
KILL ALL HUMANS!

The air in Compton's bedroom
crackled and fizzed as he,
Bryan and Samuel Nathaniel Daniels
REAPPEARED
from the twenty-seventh century.

It didn't take Compton and Bryan long to spot the gift that The Commissioner had arranged for them.

"Well?" said Samuel Nathaniel Daniels. *"What do you think?"*

What Compton thought was almost impossible to put into words. Over the last two days he had, by anyone's standards, seen some

<u>GRADE A</u>, one hundred per cent, high-speed, BUTTON-DOWN, top-quality <u>WEIRD STUFF</u>.

However, **this** was definitely the weirdest. *

* Other **WEIRD STUFF** that Compton had seen in the last couple of days included:

1. Seeing someone materialize in front of his very eyes.
2. Seeing someone disappear in front of his very eyes.
3. Seeing a man from six hundred years in the future materialize AND disappear in front of his very eyes.
4. Meeting four different versions of his father, including one who was a baby and one who was a woman.
5. Visiting a future where people used their bogeys to open secret doors.

"W-what is *that?*" stammered Compton.

"**That**," said Samuel Nathaniel Daniels, "is the very latest tool in the fight against time crime. May I introduce" – he paused dramatically – "**REPROD MODEL 101800850**, a system three, fully upgraded, robotic version of YOU."

"That is *unbelievably strange*," said Bryan.

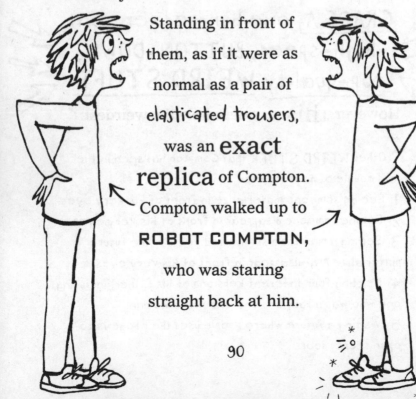

Standing in front of them, as if it were as normal as a pair of elasticated trousers, was an exact replica of Compton. Compton walked up to **ROBOT COMPTON,** who was staring straight back at him.

It was sort of like looking into a mirror, albeit a **completely crazy**, 3D mirror that had been specially designed to freak you out.

Everything about **ROBOT COMPTON** was **exactly** like Compton. It had

the **same** hair,

the **same** eyes,

was the **same** height

and was *even* wearing the **same** clothes.

"It feels so *real*," said Compton, poking **ROBOT COMPTON** gently. "What's it made of?"

"Well, its skin is made from a very complicated secret compound that has only just been developed by our top, **top scientists.** * It's the very **latest** technology. Go on, say **hello**."

* Actually the skin had been made from a combination of Bovril, jam and instant porridge that were accidentally mixed together one breakfast time in the lab.

91

Compton stood nervously in front of the robotic version of himself.

Er, h-h-*hello?*

he said cautiously.

Hello, Compton Valance, I'm **Compton Valance,**

said **ROBOT COMPTON** in a voice just like Compton's.

"Good, isn't he?" said Samuel Nathaniel Daniels eagerly. "He's exactly like you in every possible way, only he's better because he can run at five thousand miles an hour, has night vision and doesn't have a tendency to be sick on car journeys."

"Oh, come off it," said Bryan. "He can't be exactly like Compton in every single detail."

"Oh, yes he is," said Samuel Nathaniel Daniels.

"A team of sixty **FPU** agents have spent the last forty years working on him."

WHAT? yelled Bryan.

"That's *impossible*. Today is Compton's tenth birthday, how could they have been working on a robotic version of him for the last forty years?"

"Yeah, that's ridiculous," said Compton, checking the time on the clock on his bedside table. "And besides, Bravo only stole the sandwich about ten minutes ago, an event which, need I remind you, the **FPU** *didn't know* was going to happen!"

Samuel Nathaniel Daniels smiled and pointed to his **W.A.T.CH.**, tapping it meaningfully.

"Time travel, boys. Time travel."

Compton and Bryan looked at each other. "Oh yeah," they said together. "Time travel."

As soon as Bravo stole the **sandwich**, The Commissioner sent a **top secret** team of the best designers and robotic engineers back in time to 2624 to prepare a robot version of you for this EXACT moment. They worked around the clock, month after month, year after year, decade after decade, to make sure that this REPROD MODEL 101800850 was in **perfect working order** so that it could meet **any** challenge we might throw at it.

At that moment one of **ROBOT COMPTON'S** arms fell off and clanged onto the floor.

CLANG!

Well, there's one difference between you and **ROBOT COMPTON**,

smiled Bryan.

In all the time I've known you, not a single body part has ever **fallen off.**

Samuel Nathaniel Daniels quickly grabbed the arm from the floor and fixed it back onto **ROBOT COMPTON'S** shoulder.

"There," he said. "As good as new."

"Hang on," said Compton. "I've seen movies about what happens in the **FUTURE.**

Robots always go out of control and end up doing really horrible things to humans. Are you sure he'll be okay?"

"Of course he'll be okay," snorted Samuel Nathaniel Daniels. "Robot malfunctions have been *extremely rare* since THE ROBOT BATTLES OF THE TWENTY-FOURTH CENTURY."*

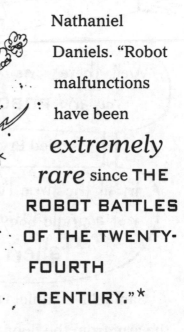

* THE ROBOT BATTLES OF THE TWENTY-FOURTH CENTURY started after a bizarre misunderstanding between an early human cyborg and a vacuum cleaner. Let's just say there were faults on both sides and thankfully no humans were hurt. It did waste a shocking amount of electricity though!

He turned and stared into the eyes of **ROBOT COMPTON.** "Now, are you clear what your instructions are?"

"Affirmative," said **ROBOT COMPTON.** "My task is to KILL ALL HUMANS, KILL ALL HUMANS, KILL KILL KILL."

Samuel Nathaniel Daniels sighed and pushed **ROBOT COMPTON'S** nose twice. Instantly, the **REPROD MODEL 101800850** powered down.

"Won't be a sec," said Samuel Nathaniel Daniels, hurriedly tapping some buttons on his **W.A.T.CH.** A moment later the air in Compton's bedroom crackled and fizzed and Samuel Nathaniel Daniels and **ROBOT COMPTON** DISAPPEARED.

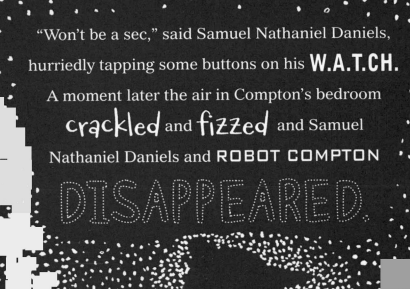

Three seconds later the air

crackled and **fizzed**

again and Samuel Nathaniel Daniels

and ROBOT COMPTON

REAPPEARED.

he said.

"My apologies for wanting to KILL you," said ROBOT COMPTON. "It will not happen again."

"Er, don't worry about it," said Compton, a little nervously.

Hey!

said Bryan.

How come I haven't got a robot version of me that wants to destroy ALL humans?

"Hold on," sighed Samuel Nathaniel Daniels as he pushed some more buttons on his W.A.T.CH.

A **ROBOT BRYAN** appeared.

There,

he said.

Happy now?

"This is *so* COOL," said Bryan.

"Will it do *anything* I want it to?"

"Of course," said Samuel
Nathaniel Daniels.

Robot Me,

commanded Bryan.

Stand on **one leg**.

ROBOT BRYAN

stood on one leg.

Bryan turned to Compton, who smiled and turned towards **ROBOT COMPTON.**

"Robot Me," commanded Compton. "Act like a baby."

WAH WAH WAH!

shrieked **ROBOT COMPTON.** "I done a plop–plop in my pot–pot."

Compton and Bryan rolled on the floor laughing.

"Ha ha, ha ha, ha ha haaah..."

"Tee hee! Hee hee hee hee..."

"Robot Me," said Bryan, trying to hold in his laughter. "Hit your head against the wall really, **really hard.**"

ROBOT BRYAN walked over to the

wall of Compton's bedroom and started

thumping away.
THUMP
THUMP
THUMP
"Amazing,"
said Compton, slowly

getting up off the floor.
THUMP
THUMP
THUMP
Bryan sat staring

with wide eyes as his

robotic self continued to

bang his head
against the wall.
THUMP
THUMP
THUMP

ROBOT BRYAN stopped bashing his head against the wall and walked back over to where **ROBOT COMPTON** was standing.

"Er, we might need to pick up the pace a little," said Samuel Nathaniel Daniels. "You know, what with **THE UNIVERSE** on the **verge** of **DESTRUCTION** and **everything**."

"What are we going to get the robots to do?" said Bryan. "Send them off on a **top secret mission** to hunt down Bravo?"

"Not *quite*," said Samuel Nathaniel Daniels. "I think we'll need them a little **closer to home.**"

COMPTON!

shouted Mr Valance from downstairs.

Stop THUMPING AROUND and get a move on. EVERYONE'S WAITING.

A look of panic spread across Compton's face.

"Oh no," he said. "My birthday party. I'd completely forgotten."

In a case of the WORST POSSIBLE TIMING EVER,

Bravo had stolen Compton's time machine sandwich on the day of Compton's tenth birthday. Naturally, when the FATE OF THE UNIVERSE is in your hands, it tends to push even the most lovely of birthday treats to the back of your mind.

Downstairs, at this very moment, there was a roomful of Compton's friends all waiting to go for a movie and a pizza.

Compton rushed to his door and opened it slightly. He could hear the hubbub of all his friends' excited chatter coming up the stairs. "What are we going to do?"

Samuel Nathaniel Daniels looked at his W.A.T.CH.

"Well, we're going to let the robots handle this," he said, before turning to ROBOT COMPTON and ROBOT BRYAN.

Can you please go downstairs for the party celebrations as instructed in POINTS 3, 42 and 117 of your CODE.

"Affirmative," said the robots. And with that, they grinned and ran off downstairs, shouting,

WE'RE COMING!

as they went.

"It's alright, I've turned off their **DEATH BLASTERS**," said Samuel Nathaniel Daniels reassuringly.

Compton and Bryan did not look at all reassured. They listened in silence as they heard everyone bustle out of Morlock Cottage and get into Mr and Mrs Valance's cars before they were driven off to enjoy some Pepperoni Fantastico at Professor Pizza.

"Right then," said Samuel Nathaniel Daniels once he was sure the coast was clear. "Now, have you any idea where Bravo might have gone first?"

"No," said Compton, walking over to his desk. "But I know where we might find out."

He opened his middle desk drawer and pulled out a HUGE, THICK book that, in Compton's own handwriting, had the words

written across the cover.

Chapter 8

The Big Book Of Mean

Compton had been writing the **Big Book Of Mean** for the last two and a half years. Recorded inside were the details of Bravo's **every** act of **cruelty** towards Compton, **every** moment of **upset** Bravo had caused him, and **every** **spiteful** word that Bravo had ever uttered.

"This is what we'll use to catch him," said Compton, as he thumbed through the pages and pages and pages of misery that Bravo had inflicted upon his person over the previous

thirty-two months,
sixteen days,
fifteen hours,
thirty-nine minutes and
four seconds.

"In here is a record of Bravo's life. If there's anything that will give us a clue as to how his mind works, and to where he might have taken the sandwich, it's in this book."

As he turned to the front of the Big Book Of Mean, Compton remembered quite clearly the very first entry he had made.

It had been the warm, sun-drenched afternoon of the

LITTLE HADRON SUMMER FETE.

Compton had been sitting at the kitchen table, making a MASSIVE model of a space rocket to enter in the Arts and Crafts section. All of a sudden, as if from nowhere, Bravo came

STORMING

into the kitchen, grabbed the space rocket, threw it on the floor and then

jumped all over it.

When Compton had gone upstairs to tell his mum about what had happened, Bravo had said that Compton had been making the rocket on the floor and that was why he'd *accidentally* trodden on it. The <u>very worst</u> bit of all, though, was that despite Compton's teary protests about how Bravo was lying, Mrs Valance had ended up believing Bravo. He remembered his mother bending down to give him a hug and saying that he needed to be a bit more careful in future. And that was when, over his mother's shoulder and out of her sight, Compton saw Bravo silently laugh and sneer at him. Even after all this time, the injustice of it burned Compton's VERY SOUL.

Look, Compton said, turning to Samuel Nathaniel Daniels.

It might not tell us EXACTLY where he is but I bet if we search hard enough we'll find a clue in here about the sort of thing Bravo will try to DO with the sandwich.

So what sort of things are we looking for? asked Bryan as he took the

Big Book Of Mean

from Compton and began to leaf through it.

I'm not sure.

Let's read some entries and see if we spot anything.

Okay, how about this, said Bryan, reading aloud from the book.

Christmas morning.

Bravo woke me up and told me Santa had been. He passed over my stocking, but when I put my hand inside it was full of cold spaghetti shapes and dead worms.

I can't be certain that Santa didn't put the spaghetti shapes and dead worms in the stocking but I'm pretty sure he didn't. Seems <u>MASSIVLY</u> out of character. Bravo laughed so hard when I put my hand in the stocking that he fell off my bed.*

* Actually, one Christmas Santa **DID** do something very similar. In 1961 he was so fed up with a particularly naughty nine year old from Russia, that he left him a stocking full of cold porridge. Santa said afterwards that the incident had been a "**HUGE error of judgement**".

This is an **extraordinary** book,

said Samuel Nathaniel Daniels.

It's like a glimpse into the mind of a teenage bully.

That's right,

said Compton.

So, let's search for **patterns** and clues. It's all we've got to go on.

Bryan flicked through the book again.

February nineteenth,

he said, stopping
at another page.

Horrible day at school.

PE was ruined because someone had messed with my white gym shorts. Some chocolate had been smeared on the inside at the back. By lunchtime, Bravo had spread a rumour that I'd had an "accident" because I was so scared of PE. I'm NOT AT ALL scared of PE and I know that it was Bravo who put the chocolate in there because it was a **Smedley's Chocolate Delight** which he loves.

Er, how did you know it was a *Chocolate Delight?*

asked Bryan s l o w l y.

Because I **tasted it**, said Compton.

It smelled **pretty delicious**, so I thought it was.

And did anyone see you sniff the brown smear at the back of your shorts and then have a lick? said Bryan.

Because **that** would probably have looked **really GROSS.**

Compton laughed.

NO, no one saw, I promise,

he said. *

* Well, no one *except* Tony Badger, who was so **grossed out** that he was **sick** all over his shoes.

So we're getting a pretty clear picture that Bravo enjoys being **really, really horrible** to you,

said Samuel Nathaniel Daniels.

What we NEED to know is what other things he likes. Imagine what he would try to do with the power to travel through time. WHAT would he want to do first?

Compton thought for a moment.

Of course, he said suddenly.

He **loves MONEY.** At the back of the **Big Book Of Mean** I've kept a record of EVERY single penny that he has stolen from me.

Samuel Nathaniel Daniels grabbed the book from Bryan and went straight to the back. Sure enough there was row after row of numbers, each relating to a specific time when Bravo had taken Compton's cash.

Thirty pence, one pound, one pound fifteen, ten pence, seventy-five pence, fifty pence, two pounds thirty. There must be a HUNDRED entries here.

152 to be precise, said Compton.

So far, Bravo owes me £186.34.

Bryan let out a long whistle.

"PHEEWWWEE...

That's a fortune,"

he said.

That's not all, said Compton, pacing around the room.

I've seen Bravo take money from Dad's change jar in the kitchen as well. He's OBSESSED with being RICH. It's all he goes on about. His dream is to be rich enough to buy ULTRA WARRIOR SCUM * so that he can impress Moira Scarfeld**. And he's always saying how amazing it would be to know what the lottery numbers are before the big Saturday night draw. Like that time when he needed Dad to get him a ticket and I thought I saw TWO Bravos.

* Bravo's favourite band.
** Bravo's favourite girl.

LOTTERY TICKET

Compton stopped dead in his tracks. Bryan and Samuel Nathaniel Daniels stared at him.

Of course, he said.

The time when I thought I saw TWO Bravos. THAT must be his first trip back in time. He'll only have taken a small bit of the sandwich because it looks so gross and stinky, so he WON'T have travelled very far back.* Why didn't I think of it sooner?

* For reasons way too complicated to go into here, the BIGGER the BITE of the TIME MACHINE SANDWICH you take, the FURTHER BACK in time you go.

Chapter 9

Bravo's First Bite
Back Through Time

The split second that he had heard

about his brother's

**TIME MACHINE
SANDWICH,**

Bravo **knew** he had to have it for himself.

It was just the thing to help him put his

genius master plan into full effect. *

After swiping the **sandwich** from

Compton's bedroom, he fired up

his laptop and printed off the

last two years of

winning lottery numbers.

* Become as rich as possible
without really doing very much.

"This is going to be *so* easy," Bravo said to himself, cackling at the thought of how rich he was going to become. All he had to do was go back in time and get his dad to buy a winning lottery ticket. Then, by the time he BURPED back, Bravo knew he would be a

MILLION-BILLION-SQUILLIONAIRE.

Despite having a brain the size of a millipede's flip-flop*, Bravo knew that he had to eat the sandwich somewhere secret.

* A particularly small millipede with tiny, tiny feet and an obsession with buying flip-flops that were at least three sizes too small.

Somewhere he wouldn't be found when he 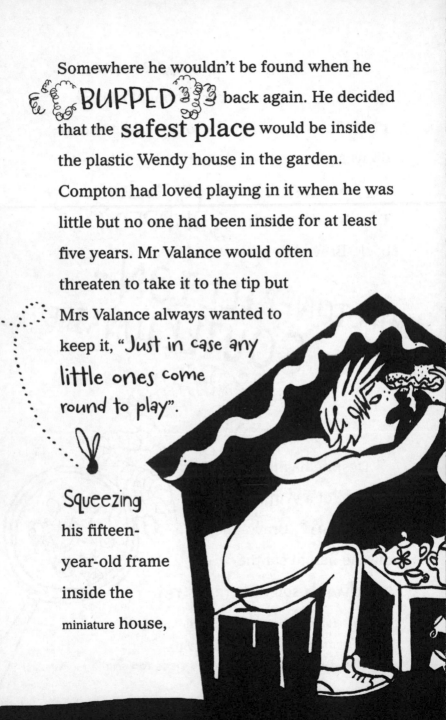 **BURPED** back again. He decided that the **safest place** would be inside the plastic Wendy house in the garden. Compton had loved playing in it when he was little but no one had been inside for at least five years. Mr Valance would often threaten to take it to the tip but Mrs Valance always wanted to keep it, "Just in case any little ones come round to play".

Squeezing his fifteen-year-old frame inside the miniature house,

Bravo squatted on the tiny chair next to the tiny table. Squished among the jumble of colour-faded plastic teapots and cups, Bravo held the sandwich up for inspection. The sunlight coming through the glassless window glinted off the rancid, disgusting sludge that oozed out of the middle of the sandwich.

Bravo pinched his nose, took the tiniest bite he possibly could and swallowed. If he could have seen himself in a mirror, he wouldn't have believed what happened next. The air in the Wendy house crackled and fizzed and Bravo became the second member of the Valance family to TAKE A TRIP THROUGH TIME.

Chapter 10

What Happened Six Months Earlier

Compton sat in the kitchen of Morlock Cottage, eating some toast and reading a comic. His father sat opposite him, sipping coffee and reading the paper.

The bassline from the title track of **ULTRA WARRIOR SCUM'S** second album,

 **"I Don't Know When You're Doing A Handstand Cos Your BREATH SMELLS LIKE YOUR BUM",**

THUMPED through the house.

Suddenly the back door flew open.

"Hi, Dad," said Bravo brightly as he walked in from the garden.

Compton narrowed his eyes. There was something about Bravo that wasn't right, something he just COULDN'T put his finger on.

"Oh, er, hi, Bravo," said his dad, a little taken aback by his son's cheery tone. He folded up his paper and placed it on the table. "I didn't know you'd gone out. I thought you were still upstairs listening to your music."

That's right,

thought Compton suspiciously.

You were upstairs, I'm sure of it.

By now, the **ULTRA WARRIOR SCUM** UWS track had become even louder, as Kent Smugglez embarked on one of his trademark fifteen-minute drum solos. *

"Oh, er, yeah," said Bravo. "I was upstairs, you know, before, but then came downstairs, er, really quietly and then I, er, went outside to look at some, er, flowers." **

Compton narrowed his already narrowed eyes even more narrowly. Something weird was going on, he could feel it.

* Kent Smugglez's drum solos were legendary.
Once, one of them went on for so long that he actually
went to sleep in the middle of it and woke up
feeling "quite refreshed".
** In case you didn't know, Bravo was
terrible at on-the-spot lying.

"Oh, okay," said Mr Valance, who also had a feeling that something very strange was happening. "Flowers. Right."

Bravo glanced at his father's paper, desperate for any clues that might tell him what the date was. The headline read:

14 D c mb r

LITTLE HADRON GAZETTE

Br ak In At N wspaper Print r
Low rcas 'E' Stol n Polic
Ar Baffl d.

The date on the paper was the fourteenth of December. Bravo had travelled back in time six months.

* The headline should have read: "Break In At Newspaper Printer. Lowercase "E" stolen. Police Are Baffled." Actually, the lower case "m" was stolen as well as the "e", but the newspaper managed to cope by turning the letter "w" upside down. Local man, Ernie Maplethorpe, was later arrested.

"So," said Mr Valance, having regained his composure. "What have you got planned for your day then?"

"Well, actually, Dad," said Bravo, taking the piece of paper with all the lottery numbers out of his pocket, "I was wondering if you'd help me with a school project?"

By now Compton's eyes had narrowed so much that they were technically shut. His inbuilt

BRAVO SUSPIC-O-METER was on FULL ALERT.

In all the years that Compton had known Bravo, he had never once asked for help with a school project.

Sorry, Bravo, said Mr Valance.

For a second I thought you asked ME to help YOU with a SCHOOL PROJECT.*

"I did," said Bravo as casually as he could, which was actually unbelievably suspiciously. "We're doing some work on numbers and probability. So I wondered if you'd go and buy me a lottery ticket?"

"A lottery ticket?" said Mr Valance. "Your school project means I have to buy you a *lottery ticket?*"

"That's right," said Bravo, checking his list of lottery numbers and then writing down the winning numbers for the next draw on a scrap of paper.

* Mr Valance's inbuilt BRAVO SUSPIC-O-METER was also on FULL ALERT.

"I would buy it myself *but* I'm not old enough." He thrust the bit of paper into his dad's hand.

The teachers said if you could get the ticket today then that would be GREAT.

Um, well, okay, if it's for a school project,

said Mr Valance. *

Compton couldn't understand it. Both he and his father *knew* something was wrong, but they couldn't quite work out what it was.

* And here we have a classic example of PARENTAL STUPIDITY. If you ask them for something – say, sweets – they will probably say no. However, if you ask them for the same thing and tell them it's part of a school project, they will fall over backwards to get it for you. (If you do plan to use this tactic, may I suggest that you say it's for a maths or science project, as ninety-nine per cent of all grown-ups have forgotten every single piece of information that they learned in school on these two subjects.)

So, what do you want me to do with the jackpot if you win?

asked Mr Valance, chuckling.

Oh, said Bravo, smiling and handing his father another piece of paper with a long number on it.

Just put it in my savings account.

Mr Valance took the piece of paper.

Oh, er, okay then, I'll be back in ten minutes,

he said, still smiling as he opened the back door. "I'll go and get the ticket, but I'm pretty sure you've got more chance of getting struck by lightning than winning the lottery. See you later."

Bravo couldn't believe it had **all** been so *easy*. The thought of what was about to happen made him go a little bit weak at the knees. As soon as he got back to his own time, he would be so *unbelievably rich* that he would

NEVER have to do anything he DIDN'T want to EVER AGAIN.

The music from upstairs suddenly stopped, which was weird because only Bravo and Compton were in the house and they were **both** in the kitchen.

The next thing Compton heard was the thump, thump, thump of clumsy feet coming down the stairs.

Without uttering another word, Bravo ran out of the house through the back door.

As it slammed SHUT behind Bravo,
Bravo came down the stairs and into the
kitchen. Compton's mouth fell to the floor.

"What are you gawping at,
LOSER?" said Bravo as he
opened the fridge, grabbed a can
of drink and went back upstairs.

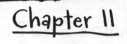

Chapter 11

The Lottery
Is Always
Such A Lottery

Back in Compton's bedroom, the air stopped

crackling and **fizzing**. Compton

and Bryan stood as still as they could, while

Samuel Nathaniel Daniels wandered

nervously around the room.

checking the display on his **W.A.T.CH.**

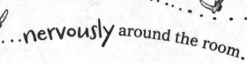

every few seconds.

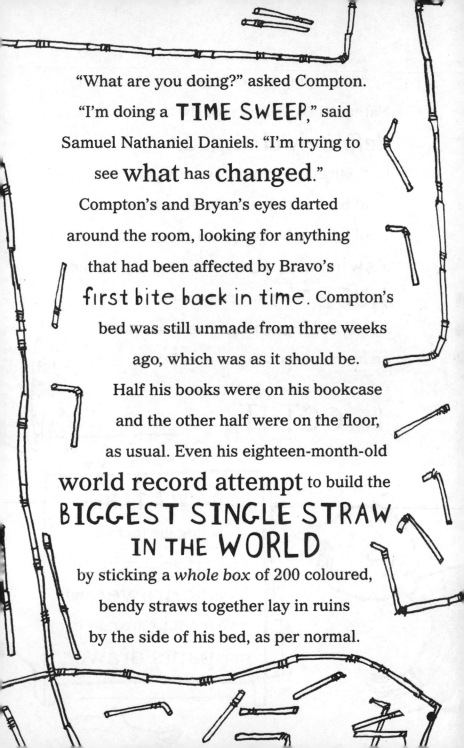

"What are you doing?" asked Compton.

"I'm doing a **TIME SWEEP**," said Samuel Nathaniel Daniels. "I'm trying to see **what** has **changed**."

Compton's and Bryan's eyes darted around the room, looking for anything that had been affected by Bravo's **first bite back in time**. Compton's bed was still unmade from three weeks ago, which was as it should be. Half his books were on his bookcase and the other half were on the floor, as usual. Even his eighteen-month-old **world record attempt** to build the **BIGGEST SINGLE STRAW IN THE WORLD** by sticking a *whole box* of 200 coloured, bendy straws together lay in ruins by the side of his bed, as per normal.

"Something *has* changed," said Samuel Nathaniel Daniels nervously. "Something *has* *definitely* changed."

"Hang on a minute," said Bryan. "If Bravo went back in time and won the lottery then wouldn't you be living in a mansion with a swimming pool and ten cars and HUGE TVs on every wall?"

Samuel Nathaniel Daniels was now on his hands and knees over by Compton's chest of drawers. "I've GOT IT," he said finally.

"My W.A.T.CH. is telling me that your pants are now in your sock drawer and your socks are now in your pants drawer."

"*Really?*" said Compton. "That's *it?* That's *all* that's *changed?*"

While Samuel Nathaniel Daniels and Compton inspected the chest of drawers, Bryan wandered over to Compton's notice board, which was hanging over his bed.

Hey, Comp, he called over his shoulder.

What's this? I haven't seen it before.

Compton went over and looked at what Bryan had found.

"It's a newspaper cutting," he said. "From six months ago."

The pair stood motionless for a moment while they read it.

T E R R Y
S K I N T P O L E,
a homeless man, was last
night celebrating becoming
one of the RICHEST MEN
IN THE WORLD, and all
thanks to the kindness of
Little Hadron resident,
Joseph Valance.

Last Thursday, Mr
Valance, 39, (pictured
above with his two sons
Bravo and Compton)
bought a lottery ticket
from Feynman's
Newsagent.

As he was walking
home Mr Valance saw
Terry Skintpole begging
for money.

ATEST MAN?

Instead of walking by, Mr Valance struck up a conversation with Terry and discovered that he had recently been left homeless after losing his job.

"I didn't have any cash to give him," explained Mr Valance to the *Little Hadron Gazette*'s reporter "But I did have the lottery ticket. I felt that Mr Skintpole had had such a run of bad luck that it was bound to change."

And change it did, as that lottery ticket won the jackpot later that evening.

Mr Skintpole offered to share the winnings with Mr Valance but Mr Valance refused, stating, "I'm just glad I could help another person who needed a leg up. The love of my wonderful family makes me rich beyond my wildest dreams."

HAS SOMEONE YOU KNOW SURPRISED THE WORLD WITH A RANDOM ACT OF KINDNESS? IF SO WE'D LIKE TO HEAR ABOUT IT. PLEASE CONTACT THE LITTLE HADRON NEWSDESK.

Compton and Bryan burst out laughing.

HA HA HA, HAH HA HA HA...

Wow, said Compton.

Bravo must have been so **unbelievably cross** when he found out that he **HADN'T** become a millionaire.

It's weird, said Bryan.

But I completely remember this happening now. It was **ALL** anyone talked about for ages. Your dad was **famous** for nearly two weeks.

Yeah, said Compton.

Do you remember that German television reporter that came over to do a bit on Dad? They kept calling him "farter" because "farter" means "father" in German, but it TOTALLY made him sound like HE'S a farter, which he IS.

Samuel Nathaniel Daniels looked worried.

This is **not good** AT ALL,

he said eventually.

Oh, **come on,** said Bryan.

The ONLY things that have happened are that Compton's pants have switched with his socks and Mr Valance has given some money to someone who needed it.

That won't be **all** that has happened,

said Samuel Nathaniel Daniels mysteriously.

That's just **all** we know about **so far**. This is only the beginning. Who knows what damage this may cause?

He's right, said Compton nervously.

Remember what The Commissioner said. Every new timeline brings the **DESTRUCTION OF THE UNIVERSE** closer and closer. We've got to find that **sandwich**.

Back in the twenty-seventh
century, behind the bogey-
activated door, in the hush-
hush, top secret operations
room, the big green clock
turned red and the number

524,160,011,520

started counting down.*

TIMELINE
NUMBER 1729
HAD
BEGUN.

* The Universe Clock counts down the minutes to
the COMPLETE AND UTTER DESTRUCTION OF
THE UNIVERSE. 524,160,011,520 minutes is one
million years and eight days.

Future Perfect Unit

Time Crime Report Sheet

 ALL FPU AGENTS MUST USE THE FOLLOWING
FORM TO REPORT ANY ROGUE TIMELINES
CREATED BY ACTS OF ILLEGAL TIME TRAVEL

Subject: Timeline 1729

Agent: Hardy-Ramanujan

PHASE ONE Description:

Subject (Bravo Valance) steals time machine sandwich
and attempts to win the lottery.

PHASE TWO Observation:

 Bravo Valance travels back in time six months and
persuades his father to buy a lottery
ticket using numbers he knows will win the jackpot.
Mr Valance buys the ticket and gives ticket to
homeless man (Terry Skintpole).

> Ticket wins £35.7 million rollover jackpot. Skintpole immediately buys top-of-the-range new car and gives car salesman a ten-thousand-pound tip.

> The car salesman uses the money to buy a round-the-world cruise trip for him and his wife. Whilst onboard, the car salesman picks his nose and flicks a bogey into the sea.

> A blue whale eats the bogey. The bogey gives the blue whale a human cold at exactly the same time as she gives birth to her babies. She passes the cold onto them and it gives them the ability to make vast quantities of snot. In time these babies have their own babies, who in time have their own babies, who have their own babies.

> With each new generation the snot-making ability gets greater and greater. Eventually, the seas and oceans of the world become almost entirely snotted over and the extra weight sends the Earth spinning off its axis. The Earth smashes into Venus, which hurtles into Mercury, which ploughs into the sun. The resulting mega explosion destabilizes the solar system and causes the Milky Way galaxy to collapse in on itself.

PHASE THREE Observation:

The resulting chain reaction of imploding galaxies causes the total and utter destruction of the universe in approximately one million years and eight days.

▶ Timeline Severity Level: **Banana**[*]

▶ Destruction of the Universe occurring in **one million years or more**

[*]All potential timelines are organized into a fruit-based coding system. Each fruit represents the amount of time left before the universe is destroyed. **Banana** represents the greatest amount of time. Next is **Papaya**. Then **Pineapple**. Then **Kiwi**. Then **Tomato**. Finally, **Tangerine** is the worst-case scenario. If a Tangerine timeline is created, the universe has just four minutes until it is destroyed. Believe me, you do not want to be around if things **"Go Tangerine"**.

Chapter 13

Smedley's Delightful Exploders

Compton and Bryan sat on Compton's bed with the **Big Book Of Mean** between them. They flicked through the pages at lightning speed, searching for clues that would help them to guess where, and more crucially **when**, Bravo would strike next.

Bryan looked up at Samuel Nathaniel Daniels, who was pacing around the room again, looking at his **W.A.T.CH.** and muttering to himself.

"It's been twenty-five minutes," Bryan said. "Surely we must know where Bravo has been by now."

"It's a very complicated process," said Samuel Nathaniel Daniels. "Only when Bravo's actions start to change the TIMELINE can we get a lock on when and where he is."

An alarm sounded on his **W.A.T.CH.**

"It's a FaceChat call," he said. "It's probably The Commissioner. *This could be it.*"

Compton and Bryan jumped off the bed and huddled around the **W.A.T.CH.** as Samuel Nathaniel Daniels hit the green TALK button.

"Hello?" he said.

ROBOT COMPTON'S face appeared on the screen.

"REPROD MODEL 101800850 requesting assistance," it said.

In the background Compton and Bryan could see all their friends running around and having fun at Professor Pizza's.

"Er, what is it, **REPROD MODEL 101800850?**" asked Samuel Nathaniel Daniels nervously. "Is everything alright?"

ROBOT COMPTON paused for a moment.

"Is it a normal human custom to eat pressed curdled liquid from cow teats, that has been covered in rind and left on a shelf for two years?"

"What?" said Bryan in disgust.

"Urgh," said Compton, pulling a face. "That sounds GROSS."

Samuel Nathaniel Daniels rolled his eyes. "Yes, 101800850, that's called cheese," he said. "It's perfectly alright to consume."

"Very well," replied ROBOT COMPTON. "How about ham and pineapple together?"

"Don't be ridiculous," said Samuel Nathaniel Daniels. "That would be disgusting."

He pushed the red button and ROBOT COMPTON'S face disappeared from the screen.

Compton and Bryan went back to the **Big Book Of Mean**. They started to flick through the pages again, shouting out things that Bravo appeared to love.

Putting worms in socks.*

Hanging people on coat hooks by their trousers.**

Making jelly with earwax.***

*Smedley's Chocolate Delights.****

* He put worms in Compton's socks.
** He hung Compton up. By his trousers. On coat hooks.
*** He made an earwax jelly for Compton to eat.
**** He stole Compton's money to buy these for himself.

WAIT! shouted Compton.

Of course, I think I know where Bravo will go next. *Smedley's Chocolate Delights* are the GREATEST LOVE of Bravo's life. They have been for years. *

Have they?

said Bryan.

* It's true. Well, almost. Smedley's Chocolate Delights are, in fact, number three on Bravo's list of greatest loves. Number one is Bravo himself and number two is Bravo's reflection in a mirror. But next are definitely Smedley's Chocolate Delights, even higher than Ultra Warrior Scum and Moira Scarfeld.

Oh yes, he has loved those chocolate bars for as long as I can remember. He's ALWAYS going on about how he dreams of being a long-lost member of the Smedley family. About how they must have POTS and POTS of cash and as many *Chocolate Delights* as they can eat.

Compton flicked through the Big Book Of Mean a little further until he came to the passage he was looking for.

Look here,

he said excitedly.

Nineteenth of September:

Bravo stood on his bed, held me by my ankles and shook all the money out of my pockets.

Then he dropped me on the floor.

Went on again about

Chocolate Delights

and how he wished he'd invented them because he'd be the richest person in Little Hadron.

I tried telling him that as they were invented over a hundred years ago, he'd also be DEAD.

He rubbed his **DIRTY PANTS** in my face after that.

> Feynman's Newsagent is the only place round here that sells **Smedley's** stuff,

said Bryan.

> That **must be** where Bravo's gone.

Ten minutes later and the bell tinkled above the front door of Feynman's shop as Compton, Bryan and Samuel Nathaniel Daniels all walked in.

> Hello, Mr Feynman,

said Compton cheerfully to a small, round man with HUGE glasses and an ENORMOUS mop of silvery hair balanced on top of his head.

Ah, Compton, said Mr Feynman.

When you see that brother of yours, will you tell him I'm getting a new shipment of *Smedley's* this afternoon?

Has he been in already today?

said Bryan.

In? *In?* chuckled Mr Feynman.

He was **in** about twenty minutes ago and wiped me out. He bought up ALL the *Chocolate Delights* that we had, PLUS another three dozen packets of popping candy.

Just then the bell above the door tinkled again. Compton, Bryan and Samuel Nathaniel Daniels spun around and watched as a man carrying a teetering pile of BIG cardboard boxes struggled through the door.

"Alright, Rich," he said to Mr Feynman. "I've got another ten boxes outside for you."

"Great," said Mr Feynman. "Just dump them by the door, I'll sort them out in a minute. People can't get enough of Smedley's. It's hard to believe they've been going for well over a HUNDRED YEARS."

The deliveryman put the boxes he was holding down and went outside to get the others.

Compton, Bryan and Samuel Nathaniel Daniels stood together and, as each one looked at the pile of boxes, their

MOUTHS DROPPED OPEN.

The label on the topmost box in the pile read:

And right there on the box, just between the lettering, was a picture of

Bravo's grinning face.

"Someone must be making a FORTUNE out of these," said Mr Feynman as he started moving the boxes to the back of the shop.

Compton ushered Bryan and Samuel
Nathaniel Daniels outside the shop so they
could talk without being heard.

When did Bravo invent those
Chocolate Exploders?

he asked.

Samuel Nathaniel Daniels tapped away at

his **W.A.T.CH.**

I can't get an EXACT date but
sometime around 1879,

he said.

So we know **where** Bravo was and
we know roughly **when,**

said Bryan.

What are we waiting for?
LET'S GO!

Samuel Nathaniel Daniels pushed some more buttons on his **W.A.T.CH.** and as the air around them crackled and fizzed they DISAPPEARED into the past.

Chapter 14

The *Smedley Confectionery Company*

The next thing they knew, Compton, Bryan and Samuel Nathaniel Daniels were in a **dark**, **dank**, **gloom-laden** street. Two sides of terraced housing loomed $HIGH$ above their heads. **Dreariness** clung to the cobbles like a used, damp rag. Compton had to hold his hand over his nose to block out the **foul, putrid stink** that seemed to come from **all** around them.

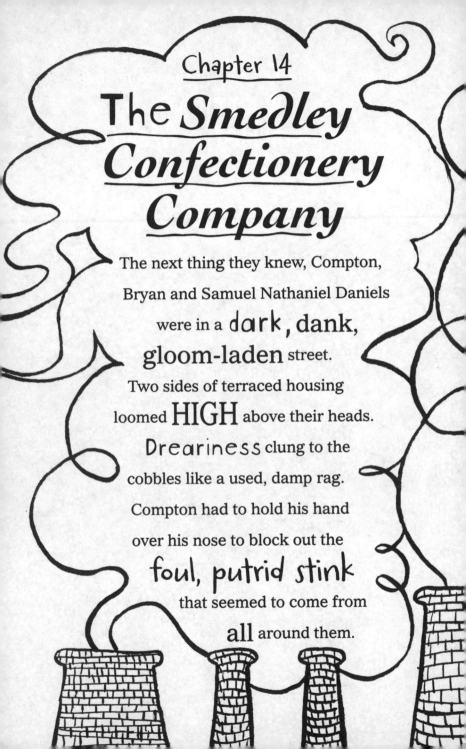

He couldn't *quite* place it but he recognized a smell like *cabbage* that had been cooking for hours and the *rasping, suffocating stench* that Bryan's grandma's dog used to make after he'd had his tea. *

If **despair** had an odour then this was **definitely IT**.

At the end of the street stood a great building of brown brick with five **ENORMOUS** chimneys **belching HUGE** plumes of **smoke** into the already darkening sky.

* To be completely fair to Mr Woofington, the stink was actually Bryan's grandma who secretly liked to break wind of an afternoon. She called it her "trumping time" and for years she successfully blamed the honk on the dog.

"There," said Samuel Nathaniel
Daniels, pointing at the foreboding building.
"It's the *Smedley's factory*.
According to my **W.A.T.CH.** it's now
March 1879. Come on, Bravo *might*
be inside."

When they reached *Smedley's*
ENORMOUS iron gates, they saw a
huge bell pull next to a sign that said:

KEEP OUT! AND STAY AWAY
BECAUSE WE WON'T LIKE YOU.
(HORRIBLE THINGS AWAIT
ANYONE WHO RINGS THIS BELL.)

Compton gulped nervously
and yanked the chain. From deep
inside the factory they heard the soft,
rhythmic tolling of the bell.

A few moments passed before a large, wooden door creaked open across the factory courtyard. From inside **Smedley's**, a figure shuffled out and walked s l o w l y towards the gate.

As the mysterious hunched figure hobbled closer and closer, Compton could see him a little better. The figure was small but stocky and had to drag his right leg behind him as he walked. He was wearing a cloak, a bit like a monk's, and a pair of clumpy work boots. His head was bowed down due to the HUGE lump that stuck out from his back, but despite his stoop, it was possible to see that he sported a great bushy beard, like a beard of bees (except it wasn't made of bees). *

* So actually, more like a *beard* beard than a *bee* beard.

When he **finally** reached the gate he put his hands on the **iron bars** and peered at the three visitors.

YYYYYYeeSSSSSSSSSS?

he said in an unusually high-pitched voice.

Compton looked at the other two.

Er, we're here to see **Bravo?** he said.

Bravo Smedley?

The **mysterious hunched** figure lifted up his head and looked Compton directly in the eye. His face was covered in **red, pus-filled boils** and his eyes were **black** and **cold** like a shark's.

WeeeellIIIIIIII,

he said, gesturing towards the factory.

You had better come inside and meet Miss Matravars.

With a metallic **clunk,**

the gates to

Smedley's Confectionery Company

s l o w l y *creaked* open.

Chapter 15

Lychett Matravars

It took a **v e r y l o n g t i m e** to get from the front gates to the factory but eventually, after a lot of shuffling and hobbling, the **mysterious** hunched man stopped outside a door with a sign that read:

> ## LYCHETT MATRAVARS,
> ### COMPANY DIRECTOR.

He knocked three times on the door and after a moment a **GREAT,** big, **DEEP** voice boomed,

COME IN.

The mysterious, hunched man opened the door s l o w l y and allowed his three guests to go into the office. Then he closed the door behind them and shuffled away down the factory corridor.

Lychett Matravars's office was large but gloomy. There was a small window that would have let some sunlight in if the sun hadn't been hidden by the clouds of smoke spewing out of the factory.

At the end of the office was a desk and behind the desk sat a woman wearing a black suit.

She looked from Bryan to Compton to Samuel Nathaniel Daniels, who removed his hat and did an extravagant bow.

"I understand you are interested in locating Bravo Smedley?" said the woman in a voice that sounded like a man's.

"Er, yes," said Compton. "How did you know *that?*"

The woman slowly stood up from her chair and moved out from behind her desk. Once her whole frame was in full view it became possible for Compton, Bryan and Samuel Nathaniel Daniels to fully appreciate her

COLOSSAL PROPORTIONS.

Everything about her was simply **GIGANTIC.** She had a **great big pointy** nose planted right in the middle of her **MASSIVE** face, and just above her putrid, **CAVERNOUS** gob perched a **mole** so plump it would have quite happily served a family of **twenty** on Boxing Day. Her **legs** resembled two **tree trunks,** which was probably a good job because the rest of her body was *so* **BIG** that it would have simply *snapped* a pair of ordinary sized legs like **chopsticks.**

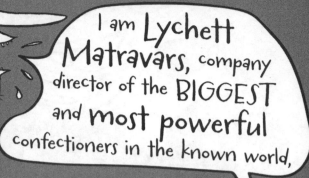

I am Lychett Matravars, company director of the BIGGEST and most powerful confectioners in the known world,

she roared.

I know EVERYTHING.

Lychett Matravars looked Compton right in the eyes with a stare so fierce Compton wondered if it would turn him into stone.

What do you want with Bravo?

she demanded.

He's my brother,

said Compton.

Oh, I get it, whispered Matravars *menacingly.*

YOU think you'll swan in here, into my beautiful factory, and try to dip your sticky little beak into the **POTS** and **POTS** of cash that I'm making, **DO YOU?**

Well... started Compton.

Well, think again, said Matravars, her death stare still trained on Compton.

You'll get **NOTHING** here. I'll tell you **EXACTLY** what I told your idiotic brother. Everything in this factory is mine. Everything that leaves this factory is mine. Everything with a *Smedley* name on it is **mine.**

As she spoke, Matravars moved steadily towards Compton until she was standing right in front of him.

"It's still **mine**, she said through her **disgusting** brown teeth.

Your brother came here with a good idea but didn't follow the **golden rule**.

Matravars walked over to a table in the corner of the office and picked up a yellowing piece of paper.

He **DIDN'T** read **the contract**.

A terrible smirk

s t r e t c h e d

across Lychett Matravars's face and mole.

179

When he showed me how to turn a *Smedley's Chocolate Delight* into a *Delightful Chocolate Exploder* I knew it would make a FORTUNE, so I made him sign this contract before we started. It gives me **everything** and him NOTHING. Oh, well, not quite nothing. In exchange for the idea and the recipe and ALL the profits, I let him put his name and portrait on the packet.

So Bravo DIDN'T get a penny,

said Compton.

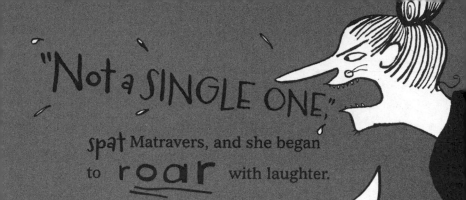

"NOT a SINGLE ONE,"

spat Matravers, and she began to roar with laughter.

You should have seen his stupid face, it was a **picture**.

Compton and Bryan started to laugh as well.

First the lottery and now THIS,

said Bryan.

Blimey, Bravo's really having a rough day, er, **century,** isn't he?

Samuel Nathaniel Daniels looked worried.

Lychett Matravars didn't like people to laugh in her company and not know why they were laughing.

"But– but– but you should be devastated," she spluttered. "Your brother hasn't made any money."

Still giggling, Bravo and Compton slowly backed towards the door with Samuel Nathaniel Daniels.

WHY AREN'T YOU DEVASTATED?

shrieked Lychett Matravars as the door to her office closed behind her visitors.

"*Quick,*" said Compton, once they were out in the corridor. "I think we need to get out of here *FAST.*"

Samuel Nathaniel Daniels punched some buttons on his **W.A.T.CH.**

I don't like this, he muttered.

I don't like this AT ALL. We need to go back to **FPU** headquarters and find out what else this timeline has **unleashed**. One thing's for sure, though – if Bravo is using the **TIME MACHINE SANDWICH** to make money, then he's going to keep on using it until he does.

Back in the twenty-seventh
century, the number on the
big red clock
changed to

48,675,002,010

and started counting down.

TIMELINE
NUMBER 235,711
HAD
BEGUN.

Future Perfect Unit

Time Crime Report Sheet

 ALL FPU AGENTS MUST USE THE FOLLOWING FORM TO REPORT ANY ROGUE TIMELINES CREATED BY ACTS OF ILLEGAL TIME TRAVEL

Subject: Timeline 235,711

Agent: Goldblach

PHASE ONE Description:

Subject (Bravo Valance) takes popping candy back to the nineteenth century in an attempt to become a rich businessman.

PHASE TWO Observation:

> By taking popping candy back to the nineteenth century, Bravo Valance commits a breach of the First Law Of Time. *

* The **ILOT** states that in order to maintain a sterile travelling environment **no foodstuffs** shall be taken from the future to the past.

> The chocolate bars he creates are so delicious that the Smedley Confectionery Company are unable to keep up with demand.

> Their supply of popping candy is soon used up, which leads to Lychett Matravers setting up an experimental laboratory to try to recreate the popping candy.

> After ten years of continuous experimentation the laboratory accidentally creates a material that is called SUBSTANCE X.

> Unable to find a use for it, SUBSTANCE X is put in a box and stored in a loft belonging to the scientists.

> Ten years pass by before a rat nibbles her way into the box and uses it for her home.

> The rat soon becomes infected with SUBSTANCE X and dies but the fleas on her back survive and, over time, absorb SUBSTANCE X into their own genetic make-up.

> Over the course of the next eighty thousand years the fleas mutate into giant killer fleas

that are able to travel faster than the speed
of light, and decide to take over the world.

> Humans are no match for them and so once
the fleas conquer Earth they set about trying
to conquer other worlds.

> Over the next few years they move from planet
to planet, from star system to star system,
until they become the dominant species in the
universe. Unfortunately, due to their unique
DNA structure, whenever a flea dies it creates a
black hole.

> Eventually millions upon millions of black holes
begin to eat away at the fabric of the universe.

PHASE THREE Observation:

The creation of the race of super-fast killer
fleas leads to the destruction of the universe in
approximately one hundred thousand years.

▶ Timeline Severity Level: **Pineapple**

▶ DOU* **in one hundred thousand years or less**

* Destruction of Universe

Chapter 17

Bravo's Last Bite
Back In Time

The air inside the Wendy house in the garden
of Morlock Cottage

crackled and **fizzed**

and Bravo **APPEARED**, bashing his
knees on the tiny plastic table. For a fifteen-
year-old boy with a **TIME MACHINE** it
was proving remarkably difficult for Bravo
to become

RICH
beyond his
WILDEST DREAMS.*

* Although he seemed more than capable of
DESTROYING THE UNIVERSE.

Bravo kicked over the table in **frustration**, then the tiny chair, then he threw a tiny teacup at the wall and knocked over the teapot. It was a **most** *unsatisfying* **RAMPAGE.**

"What is going **wrong?**" Bravo muttered to himself.

I mean, it's not asking a lot, is it? All I WANT is to become the richest fifteen year old in the world using a sandwich that helps me travel through TIME.

Suddenly* a **brilliant**** idea **flashed***** across Bravo's mind like a herd of **wild stallions****** racing***** across the plains. ******

It was true Bravo wanted to become

STUPENDOUSLY **wealthy** without actually having to bother doing **anything** but a quick glance at his **top three** list of things he **most wanted** in the world showed that money wasn't the only thing he craved. *******

* Slowly.
** Average.
*** Meandered.
**** A slumber of sloths.
***** Crawling.
****** Along the branch of a Cecropia tree.
******* This list **DID** exist. He kept it inside a sock that he kept inside an empty pizza box that he kept under a pile of clothes that was hidden under his bed. ⟶

TOP THREE THINGS I WANT
by Bravo Valance

M4B

1. BECOME **SO rich** that I can buy ULTRA WARRIOR SCUM and fire lead singer REx Blaxx. Then I can get the band to record my NEW songs. The album would include "MY Favourite Thing IS Farting IN Your Face" and "The BEST Bit about You IS the Back Of Your Head". →

UWS

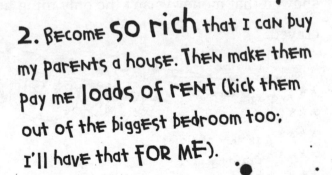

2. BECOME **SO rich** that I can buy my parents a house. Then make them pay me **loads of rent** (kick them out of the biggest bedroom too; I'll have that FOR ME).

3. BECOME worshipped like a GOD.

Yes, it was this last point on the list that was

firing Bravo's imagination.

He didn't need to become rich to become worshipped. Surely anyone with the knowledge of life in the twenty-first century would be thought of as godlike if they went far enough back in time. Imagine showing people a wheel before the wheel had been invented. Or a bucket. Or an individually-wrapped, lemon-scented handwipe. It would

BLOW THEIR MINDS!

He just needed to travel far enough back.

Taking the TIME MACHINE SANDWICH in his hand, Bravo held it up to inspect it properly. It oozed and SQUELCHED between his fingers.

GREAT GLOBS OF SLIME

dripped out of the stinking bread
onto the floor of the Wendy house.

Bravo couldn't take his eyes off it.

Enchanted by its strange magnificence,
he kept staring and staring. The more
he stared, the more he recognized the
beauty in the swirling, fizzing
awfulness of the decomposing

sandwich.

And then,

as if he was in

some kind of

hypnotic trance,
Bravo put a HUGE

corner of the

sandwich in his

mouth and took the most

ENORMOUS BITE.

194

The air in the Wendy house
crackled and fizzed
and Bravo DISAPPEARED.

Little did he or anyone else know

that it would be

HIS
LAST BITE
OF THE
SANDWICH.

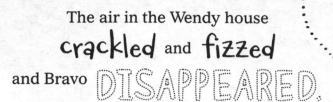

Future Perfect Unit

Copyright © 2565 The Future Perfect Unit Site powered by W.A.T.CH. Precision Systems

Time Crime Report Sheet

> ALL FPU AGENTS MUST USE THE FOLLOWING
> FORM TO REPORT ANY ROGUE TIMELINES
> CREATED BY ACTS OF ILLEGAL TIME TRAVEL

Subject: Timeline 1296

Agent: Yahtzee

PHASE ONE Description:

Subject (Bravo Valance) takes enormous bite from sandwich and ends up travelling back in time to the year 526,210 BCE.

PHASE TWO Observation:

> Bravo travels back to the time when early humans called Homo heidelbergensis * lived.

* **Homo heidelbergensis** were a descendent of the earlier **Homo erectus** and an ancestor of **Homo sapiens**, i.e. us.

> After gaining the trust of the tribe leader (who he renames Iain), Bravo teaches them the things that he believes will make them think he is a god.

> First he teaches them how to "drum like a rock star". This involves hitting tree trunks, stones and the heads of other Homo heidelbergensis as hard and rhythmically as possible.

> Bravo also shows them how to "spin their sticks" and toss them in the air at the end of a performance. Next he teaches them how to do the perfect armpit-fart.*

> After that, Bravo teaches the Homo heidelbergensis to burp and talk at the same time. After he imparts all of this, the early humans do indeed think he is a god.

> The result of Bravo's trip back to pre-history means that rock music is invented nearly half a million years earlier than it should have been.

* Bravo really was world-class in this sphere, having recently completed a lifetime dream to **armpit-fart** all nine of **Beethoven's** symphonies.

> This dependency on rock music at such an early stage in human development leads to human brains becoming much smaller than they would have been.

> The smaller-brained humans become proficient at building enormous stadiums and ripping holes in their clothes.

> In 2999, an attempt to break the World Record for the high-kick air-guitar move, known as the Van Halen, ends in disaster.

> Nearly two-thirds of the world's 74 billion people attempt this move at the same time. The result of nearly 50 billion people all jumping up and down at the same time in extremely tight trousers is a thermonuclear explosion that causes a black hole to instantly rip through the solar system.

PHASE THREE Observation:

> The result of having a brand new black hole in the solar system is catastrophic.

> The black hole creates a tunnel from one end of the universe to the other. This tunnel allows marauding gangs of aliens through and plunges the galaxy into a hundred years of interplanetary warfare.

> During the second phase of these wars, a machine of great power and destruction is created by harnessing the energy of the sun.

> When the machine is used, it sets off an explosion that destroys the universe. This will happen in approximately five thousand years.

▶ Timeline Severity Level: **Kiwi**

▶ DOU in **five thousand years or less**

Chapter 19

THE SOMBRERO
OF INVISIBILITY

Meanwhile, back in the twenty-seventh century, the door marked → INVISIBILITY RESEARCH CENTRE opened and thirty giggling, excited school children tumbled out into the Theodore Logan Memorial Hall and Reception Zone.

A slightly frazzled-looking Agent Hendrix followed them. "Ellery Shabbington?" she called. "*Ellery?* Has **anyone** seen Ellery Shabbington? She was here a minute ago."

Agent Hendrix sighed. <Sigh>

"Why does this **always** happen on **my** school tours? I tell them **not** to touch anything but they always want to try on

THE SOMBRERO OF INVISIBILITY."

Agent Hendrix shook her head, pushed a button on her **W.A.T.CH.** and spoke into it.

Hi, Jan, this is Hendrix in Theodore Logan, she said.

I've got a school tour and we've got a problem... Yeah, uh-huh, how did you guess? ...Yeah, the SOMBRERO AGAIN... I know, it's the TENTH TIME it's happened... Uh-huh... Yes, there's a WARNING sign right next to it but I think we might have to change it... Er, I think it says

PLEASE **DO NOT TOUCH** THE REALLY COOL FUN HAT THAT WILL GIVE YOU AWESOME POWERS

Yeah, you're right. We should really change the sign. I'll mention it to Pete.

Agent Hendrix pushed another button on her **W.A.T.CH.** and turned to the rest of the children. "Alright then, let's have some lunch. Follow me and **nobody else** touch **anything**, okay?"

As the party trooped off to the **FPU** canteen, they passed a cleaner trying to open a plain door with a sign that said

COMPLETELY
ORDINARY
BROOM
CUPBOARD

Open up,

he said, yanking on the handle and **BANGING** on the door.

I just **saw you** go in there. Please, I just need to get a broom.

"Oh, that cupboard is out of action," said a mysterious woman wearing a T-shirt that simply said EMPLOYEE on the front. She seemed to have appeared out of nowhere. "There are no brooms in there today and there most certainly isn't a hush-hush top secret operations room behind that door."

The cleaner looked suspiciously at the mysterious woman.

"I just saw three people going in there," he said.

"I think you are mistaken," said the mysterious woman in a REALLY mysterious way. "But if you follow me, I can show you where the brooms are kept."

And with that, the mysterious woman led the cleaner through a door marked:

MEMORY
WIPING
AREA

Chapter 20

Teaching The Ancient Britons How To Blow Snot Bubbles

Inside the hush-hush top secret operations room and behind the door activated by bogeys that was behind the door marked COMPLETEY ORDINARY BROOM CUPBOARD, things were getting really busy.

New TIMELINES were being activated with increasing speed and regularity. Every few minutes a flashing light would appear above an agent and they would shout out their timeline number.

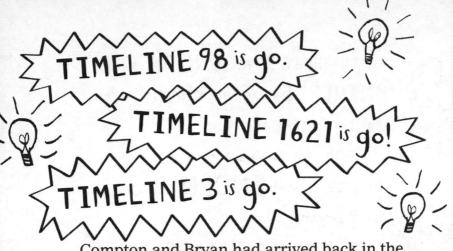

TIMELINE 98 is go.

TIMELINE 1621 is go!

TIMELINE 3 is go.

Compton and Bryan had arrived back in the operations room a few moments before and were standing with The Commissioner on the metal balcony. They looked down on the **thousands** of agents and watched with increasing anxiety as the **TIMELINES** kept changing. Samuel Nathaniel Daniels had been sent off to find some nice biscuits.

"**Look,**" said Bryan, pointing to the **UNIVERSE CLOCK**.

"It's going **mad.**"

With each new **TIMELINE**, the number on the clock kept changing.

"The time until the END OF THE UNIVERSE is getting shorter and shorter," said Compton.

"Yeah, but don't worry though, that number is still ENORMOUS," said Bryan.

The UNIVERSE CLOCK read:

1,760,160,000

"That's the number of minutes until the END OF THE UNIVERSE," said The Commissioner. "I'd say we've got about three and a half thousand years."

The bottom of Compton's feet suddenly felt very prickly.

TIMELINE 124 is go,

shouted an agent.

The readout on the **UNIVERSE CLOCK** changed to:

1,452,160,000

"*Actually*, make that about two and a half thousand years until **THE END OF THE UNIVERSE**," said The Commissioner.

WHAT'S GOING ON?

shouted Compton.

WHY is everything changing so fast? WHY can't we catch Bravo?

Well, to be honest, we just don't know,

said The Commissioner, pacing up and down the length of the balcony.

In the last ten minutes Bravo has COMPLETELY CHANGED the history of the HUMAN RACE, 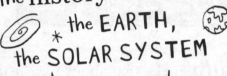 the EARTH, the SOLAR SYSTEM and THE UNIVERSE.

Bravo managed to get William the Conqueror on the English throne ten years *earlier* than he should have been when he showed him how to give a **perfect wedgie.**

He brought forward global climate change by three hundred years when he went back two billion years and dumped a fully loaded chilli kebab still in its polystyrene box into the sea.

And he caused the INTERGALACTIC WAR OF THE TWENTY-SECOND CENTURY when he went back and showed the Ancient Britons how to blow snot bubbles.

The Commissioner stopped pacing up and down.

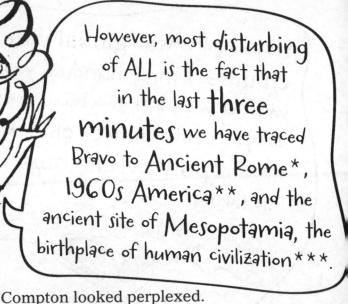

However, most disturbing of ALL is the fact that in the last **three minutes** we have traced Bravo to Ancient Rome*, 1960s America**, and the ancient site of **Mesopotamia**, the birthplace of human civilization***.

Compton looked perplexed.

But that's **impossible,** he said.

The sandwich ONLY takes you back in time to the same place you're already in!

* Where he managed to make Julius Caesar the Roman Emperor fifteen years early by showing him how to cheat at cards.
** Where he set back the moon landings by thirty-two years by pushing a button marked DO NOT PUSH on the Apollo 11 rocket.
*** Where he taught the industrious settlers of the Euphrates river how to "kick back and party".

"*I know,*" said The Commissioner. "**Something** has changed that has given Bravo the opportunity to travel to any time in the past and any place. We need to catch him fast, Compton – time is running out for all of us."

Compton didn't say anything, but on the inside he felt **terrible**. It was *his* TIME MACHINE SANDWICH and *his* brother that were going to cause the

DESTRUCTION OF THE UNIVERSE

and he couldn't seem to do anything about it.

However, at that **precise moment**, just as hope seemed to be slipping away, a germ of a seed of an idea was beginning to form inside Compton's brain.

An idea that could SAVE THE UNIVERSE.

Chapter 21

The Sandwich Bites Back!

What had happened to Bravo was actually quite simple. When he had gone back to the *Smedley Confectionery Company* in 1879, he accidentally, and completely unknowingly, spilled a small amount of **popping candy** into the **TIME MACHINE SANDWICH**.

The carbon dioxide and sugar molecules in the popping candy mixed with the carbon and hydrogen molecules bubbling within the TIME MACHINE SANDWICH.

This new chemical reaction completely changed the time travelling properties of the sandwich. The sandwich was now capable of transporting Bravo to any place in the past as well as any time.

The **sandwich's** altered chemical make-up also meant that each time Bravo **BURPED,** instead of returning to his present, he would travel to a **NEW MOMENT IN TIME.**

Whereas before, Bravo had been in control of **when** and **where** he would go, now **the sandwich** was in control. **IT HAD BITTEN BACK.**

Bravo was alone, hurtling through TIME and SPACE, with absolutely no way of knowing WHERE he would END UP.

And each new trip brought THE UNIVERSE closer to the

BRINK OF DESTRUCTION.

It was not ideal at all.

Chapter 22

CODE TANGERINE! REPEAT, CODE TANGERINE!

The floor of the HUSH-HUSH TOP SECRET OPERATIONS ROOM was now a blur of activity and a

DEAFENING ROAR of

NOISE.

Every few seconds, a new TIMELINE was being started and nobody seemed to know what was *really* going on.

The ⟩YELLS⟨ from the agents got
louder and **louder** and the readouts
on the UNIVERSE CLOCK were getting
lower
and
lower.
The DIN was so DEAFENING that
Compton could hardly make himself heard.

I'VE GOT TO GO
AFTER BRAVO,

he yelled to The Commissioner.

I'm sure there's something I've
missed. If I can just go back and look
in the Big Book Of Mean,
I'll find something.

No can do, I'm afraid,

said The Commissioner.

Every time Bravo changes the past it has HUGE effects on the rest of TIME. With every new TIMELINE created, the rest of history gets more jumbled up. Travelling through time NOW would be incredibly dangerous.

Back from his hunt for biscuits, Samuel Nathaniel Daniels stepped forward awkwardly.

We could send him back if we had a specific date and time, couldn't we?

he said nervously.

What would happen if you had a specific date and time?

said Compton.

The Commissioner answered Compton but **stared hard** at Samuel Nathaniel Daniels.

The tiny, weeny **germ** of a **seed** of an **idea** in Compton's brain was starting to grow now.

We just have to hope that Bravo doesn't trigger **TIMELINE 42,**

said The Commissioner.

Why not? asked Bryan.

"**Well,**" said The Commissioner, "we **know** that every timeline **except one** will bring about **THE DESTRUCTION OF THE UNIVERSE,** right?"

Right, said Compton and Bryan.

The Commissioner continued, "Well, most TIMELINES don't bring about the END OF THE UNIVERSE for hundreds of thousands of years. However, some TIMELINES see the END OF THE UNIVERSE happening in a few thousand years. Some even less than that. But by far the WORST SCENARIO we have to contend with is TIMELINE 42. When TIMELINE 42 happens, the whole room will start flashing red, alarms will go off and we will be in a CODE TANGERINE SITUATION."

Suddenly the whole of the HUSH-HUSH TOP SECRET OPERATIONS ROOM started to flash red and great, noisy alarms started to sound.

TIMELINE 42,

yelled an agent.

A mechanical voice cut through the **racket** of the alarms.

ATTENTION, ATTENTION, WE ARE NOW IN A CODE TANGERINE SITUATION! REPEAT, A CODE TANGERINE SITUATION.

How long have we got?

asked Compton.

You DON'T want to know,

said The Commissioner.

Chapter 23

Just How Bad Could TIMELINE 42 Be?

REALLY BAD.

Chapter 24

What Triggered
TIMELINE 42

The last few minutes/almost three thousand years* had been very weird for Bravo. He wasn't quite sure what was going on, but since he had ﹛BURPED﹜ back from his dreadful time with Lychett Matravers at the *Smedley Confectionery Company*, things had suddenly become really, really, really strange.** He was feeling very dizzy and a bit sick from the recent speed and frequency of his leaps through TIME.

* Depending on your point of view.
** Really.

So, when the air stopped fizzing and crackling around him, Bravo decided he would take a little time to examine his new surroundings.

He had to strain his eyes to see but it appeared as though he was in a perfectly quiet and very dark kitchen. He stood for a moment and let the calm wrap its arms around him. The only light came from a candelabra flickering on a table in the centre of the room.

Eventually, fighting against his desire to be sick on the floor, Bravo staggered over to the table with his arms stretched out in front of him like a zombie.

"I **don't** want to do this any more," he moaned, grabbing the candelabra so that he could use it to have a proper look around.

Bravo held the candelabra high in the air and saw that the kitchen was **ENORMOUS**. Right in front of him, and taking up a whole wall, was a **GIGANTIC** fireplace. In the grate, Bravo made out the faint glow of dying embers. To the right of the fireplace, he saw a **BIG** shelf piled high with pots that looked like cauldrons. On the opposite side of the room was another wooden table that **groaned** under the weight of **dozens** and **dozens** of delicious-looking **pies**.

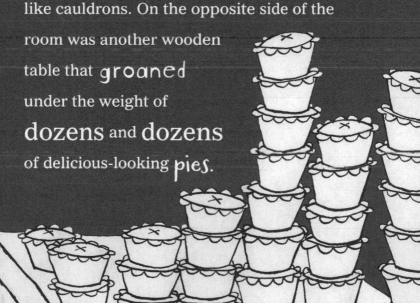

There were few people in the world that loved to scoff a pie as much as Bravo, but on this occasion he resisted. His stomach was still doing somersaults from his recent time travelling and he just knew that eating a pie from history would only end badly.

Looking around some more, Bravo saw a large wooden door in the corner of the room and next to it, on a hook, hung a BIG, thick cloak. Despite the warm embers of the fire the kitchen was bitterly cold, so Bravo went over to the hook, grabbed the cloak and wrapped it around him. The cloak had a hood, which he pulled tightly over his head. Then, he slowly pushed open the door and felt the bracing kiss of COLD NIGHT AIR.

Once he stepped outside, Bravo looked around and was **mightily** impressed. It appeared that he was in some kind of castle.

Whoever it belonged to must have been **amazingly important** because it was **ENORMOUS.** As he looked around, Bravo had a **funny feeling** that he had been here **before,** or at least had seen it on TV.*

* Most of Bravo's historical knowledge came from accidentally seeing it on TV because he couldn't be bothered to get up and change the channel.

Even though night had fallen, the castle was **alive** with activity. Some men *raced* around holding torches, while others huddled in corners and whispered secrets to each other. Suddenly a voice shouted from across the courtyard.

YOU! I SAY, YOU!

No one responded.

YOU. YOU. YOU!

shouted the voice again.

Me? said Bravo nervously.

Yes, YOU,

said a man, emerging from the shadows.

Are you the physician* we sent for?

* In case you didn't know, "physician" is another name for doctor.

Er, *physician?*

said Bravo a bit more nervously.

Aye, man, physician,

said the man impatiently.

We have NO time for games. YOU are wearing the physician's cloak. Therefore YOU must be the physician we sent for.

He grabbed Bravo by the shoulder.

Come now, he said urgently.

There is precious little time. King Henry is sick and we need your counsel.

Before Bravo knew what was **happening,** the man had bundled him a c r o s s the courtyard, through a **HUGE** door, down a **narrow** corridor,

through a series of **heavy** doors,  **UP** a flight of stairs, along another **narrow** corridor,

through a **HUGE** room, then another

HUGE ROOM

down another **narrow** corridor, **down** some stairs, through another **HUGE** door, **UP** some **more** stairs

...and into **a room** where he was confronted with a row of faces all staring expectantly at him.

"I have the physician," announced the man who Bravo had met in the courtyard.

On hearing this, another man wearing a white shirt and a red velvet cloak stepped forward. From across the room, the man looked **deep** into Bravo's eyes. Bravo felt a chill **roll down his spine.**

"*Physician?*" cried the man. "**Pah**, he is just a boy. **Tell me,** *boy,* what is your name?"

"Bravo," said Bravo.

"*Bravo?*" said the man. "I have **never** heard of such a name."

"Wh-who are **you?**" Bravo **stuttered.**

A **gasp** went around the room.

The man in the red cloak walked closer
to Bravo, **never once** dropping his
steely gaze. When he stopped, he leaned
in menacingly.

I am the Duke of
Suffolk, brother-in-law to
King Henry and Lord
High Steward,

he spat.

Tell me, boy,
can you cure the king?

I-I-I don't know,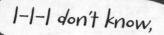

stammered Bravo, still not really knowing **what on earth** was going on.

Well, said the Duke of Suffolk, smiling like a **crocodile** and guiding Bravo through an open doorway,

let me give you an **incentive**. Unless you cure him, **you** will **LOSE. YOUR. HEAD.** You have **ONE HOUR.**

The door shut behind Bravo with a **THUD** and he heard a **HUGE** metal bolt lock him inside.

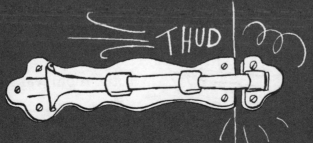

THUD

Chapter 25

Revenge Is As Sweet As A Really, Really Strong Mint

Bravo turned from the locked door and examined the room he had been shoved into. The walls flickered with eerie shadows cast by a dozen candles' dancing flames. In one corner, a hideously ugly woman was sitting in a BIG bucket and rubbing leaves in her hands.

At the end of the room was a

HUGE four-poster bed and on the bed, quite motionless, lay a **fat, bearded man** who Bravo assumed to be King Henry.

Next to the bed a lady kneeled in prayer, only stopping when she noticed Bravo.

She looked him up and down.

"Are you the **physician?**" she asked softly.

Bravo could feel **butterflies** gathering in his stomach.

"Er, yeah, I **guess** I am," he replied.

"What is '**Farting Up My Noseholes**'?" she enquired politely.

Bravo looked down and saw that the cloak he had borrowed had come loose and his favourite **ULTRA WARRIOR SCUM** badge was on display.

"Er, it's kind of *tricky* to explain," said Bravo. *

The old woman in the bucket cackled and threw a jar of **fish guts** over her head.

"Pray, **master physician**," the lady said gently, reaching out her hands towards him, "I beg you to help our king."

* Farting Up My Noseholes was the name of **ULTRA WARRIOR SCUM**'s first British tour.

The kind lady led Bravo by the hand over to where the king was resting. The king was asleep and snoring like a pig that had swallowed a lawnmower.

As Bravo drew nearer he was able to take in the king's ENORMOUS frame. His stomach was the biggest that Bravo had *ever* seen and on his face he sported a BIG, bushy, red beard.

"It's <u>Henry the Eighth</u>," Bravo gasped. "I'm in the *same room* as HENRY THE EIGHTH."

"*Pardon?*" said the kind lady.

"Oh, nothing," said Bravo.

He prodded the king in the belly.

I'm poking Henry the Eighth,

ZZZZZZ...

he said, giggling.

"*Sorry?*" said the kind lady.

"Oh, nothing," said Bravo again.

The old woman in the bucket suddenly cracked three eggs on her head and shouted

DOOM!

very loudly.

The kind lady lowered her voice.

The wise woman has been trying for two days, she said.

But NONE of her cures appear to do ANYTHING for the king.

Er, what's wrong with him? asked Bravo.

We do not know, she said.

Some say 'tis gout and others say he has the **sweating sickness.**

The kind lady started to sob.

And what has *she* given him?

said Bravo, pointing to the wise woman.

Oh, the usual,

the kind lady replied, drying her eyes.

A mixture of herbs and a hangman's rope pressed against his head. But to NO AVAIL.

At that the **wise woman** let out a **howl** and began rubbing mud and leaves onto her tongue.

Bravo thought that the word "wise" perhaps **wasn't** the best description for her. Maybe "batty" or "crackers" would have been more suitable.

"What medicines do you have?" asked the kind lady. "I shall wake the king so you can administer your potions."

With that, the kind lady began shaking the shoulder of King Henry and slapping his face.

Bravo didn't know what he was going to do – he **didn't** have any medicines at all. NO potions or lotions, NO pills or bandages or splints or *anything.*

"WH-WHO WAKES THE KING?" shouted King Henry in a feeble voice.

"'Tis the physician sent by Suffolk," said
the kind lady. "He has travelled far and has
come to give you his special medicine."

The king sat up with some difficulty.
His stomach was so ENORMOUS
that this took quite a long time. When he was
upright, with some pillows behind his back,
he looked Bravo straight in the eye.

"Well," he said, sniffing and wiping
his nose on his sleeve, "I am waiting."

Bravo could hear that the king was
a bit bunged up and snuffly.

He's probably just got a cold,
he thought to himself.

"Still waiting,"
said the king,
sniffing
again before
sneezing.

Bravo had to think quickly and that was not one of his strong points.

The king turned to the kind lady. "Tell me, Elizabeth, are the EXECUTIONERS' AXES all sharpened and ready for action?"

"Father," said Elizabeth. "Don't tease the physician." Bravo couldn't believe it. Not only was he in a room with KING HENRY THE EIGHTH, but he was also in a room with a woman who was called Elizabeth. Just like his mum.*

* Bravo's brain was currently running at its maximum capability so he didn't realize that he was actually in a room with King Henry the Eighth and the future Elizabeth the First (well, the past Elizabeth the First, but you get the idea).

"Physician," said the king. "You are trying my patience. Do you have medicine for me or _not?_"

Bravo rubbed his hands over his pockets and with great relief felt something hard.

"Yes," he said, pulling out a half-eaten packet of

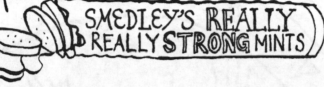

"Here's my special medicine."
Bravo took a REALLY, REALLY STRONG MINT from the pack and gave it to the king.

The king held the REALLY, REALLY STRONG MINT between his thumb and forefinger. He held it up to the light and examined it like it was a rare and very precious jewel.

"Put it in your mouth and suck," said Bravo.

The king s l o w l y brought the mint closer and closer to his mouth, **never once** taking his eyes off it, and then

popped it on his tongue.

Aaaaaaaaahhhhhhh!

he **yelled** as the mint made contact with his tastebuds.

"WHAT MANNER OF DEVIL MEDICINE HAVE YOU GIVEN HIM?" shouted Elizabeth as she watched her father **leap** out of bed and **run around** the room at top speed, **yelling** and **screeching** as he did so.

All the commotion had obviously been heard outside, as Suffolk and some guards unlocked the door and rushed in.

"WHAT IS GOING ON?" bellowed Suffolk as he stood in amazement and watched King Henry dash **round** and **round** the room, flapping his arms as he went.

My. Mouth. Is. On. Fire!

he called out on each lap, before finally running out of

s t e a m

and falling onto the bed in a heap.

"Father!" Elizabeth ran over to where the king lay.

"GUARDS!" yelled Suffolk, pointing at Bravo. "Arrest him for treason. He has murdered the king. He must be tried and EXECUTED NOW!"

The guards raced over and grabbed Bravo.

TAKE YOUR HANDS OFF HIM!

screamed King Henry from face down on his bed.

"M-m-my lord?" stammered Suffolk.
"You are ALIVE!"

The king pushed himself off the bed, stood up properly and took a l o n g, deep sniff.

Of course I am ALIVE, you flagon of donkey spittle, and I feel fantastic.

Suffolk looked nervously at Bravo.

"Tell me, physician," said the king, "what is in that REMARKABLE medicine of yours?"

Oh, I really couldn't say,

said Bravo, pretending to be modest but also being very honest at the same time.

"Well, sir, I haven't felt this good in a
long, l o n g time," said the king,
SLAPPING Bravo on the back.

"You must be rewarded. Name your prize.

Money... jewellery... land...

Whatever **you** desire is **yours**."

"Well," said Bravo, looking *slyly* at the
Duke of Suffolk, "I've always *rather liked*
Suffolk. We used to go there on our holidays."

The king turned and looked at his
brother-in-law and Lord High Steward.
He narrowed his eyes and smiled.

Very well,
he said.
The county of Suffolk shall be yours. Everyone, pray give three cheers for the new Duke of Suffolk.
Hip hip...
Hooray!
Hip hip...
Hooray!
Hip hip...
Hooray!

Future Perfect Unit

Time Crime Report Sheet

> ALL FPU AGENTS MUST USE THE FOLLOWING
> FORM TO REPORT ANY ROGUE TIMELINES
> CREATED BY ACTS OF ILLEGAL TIME TRAVEL

Subject: Timeline 42

Agent: Adams

PHASE ONE Description:

Subject (Bravo Valance) travels back to the court of Henry the Eighth and is given the title of Duke of Suffolk.

PHASE TWO Observation:

> After becoming the Duke Of Suffolk, Bravo stays in Tudor England and marries Elizabeth. When King Henry dies, Bravo is placed on the throne and becomes King of England.

> At the same time an asteroid the size of Wales starts moving on a collision course with the sun. The collision won't happen for over one thousand years but an advanced alien race has decided that it should help out humanity.

> They send a spaceship with instructions to destroy the asteroid before it reaches the sun. However, in observing the Earth, the aliens see the foil wrapper from the packet of SMEDLEY'S REALLY, REALLY STRONG MINTS.

> The aliens think that humans are four hundred years more advanced than they really are and so must have everything under control and do not need help.

PHASE THREE Observation:

When the asteroid hits the sun, the resulting chain causes the instant and total destruction of the universe on Saturday the twenty-third of April, 2664, at 4.14 p.m. (On the plus side, it looks unbelievably spectacular.)

▶ Timeline Severity Level: **Tangerine**

▶ DOU in **four minutes or less**

Chapter 27

Saturday the twenty-third of April, 2664, at 4.10 p.m.

Compton looked at the BIG red clock hanging from the ceiling of the hush-hush top secret operations room at FPU HQ.

260

A mechanical voice **boomed** around the room:

THREE MINUTES UNTIL THE END OF THE UNIVERSE!

Sorry,

said The Commissioner.

Three minutes.

But...but there has to be **something** we can **do,**

said Compton.

Yeah, agreed Bryan.

We can't just sit around doing **NOTHING.**

Oh, I'm not going to do
NOTHING,

said The Commissioner.

First of all I'm going to
PANIC,
then I'm going to flap
and then I'm going to run
round and round
and round in a circle.

Wait! said Compton suddenly.

The germ of an idea in his brain was growing and growing.

You know you said you could create a TIME BUBBLE around a specific moment in the past?

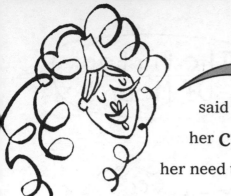

Yes?

said The Commissioner,
her **curiosity** overtaking
her need to **flap** for a moment.

Well, how long would
it take to set up?

If it's in the **past**, no time
at all. We just need to input
the time and date into our
supercomputer. **Why?**

I've got an **idea,**

said Compton.

I made a book where I've
written down **every time**
Bravo has been **horrible** to me.

The Big Book Of Mean?

said Bryan.

Yes,

said Compton.

A mechanical voice boomed
around the room:

TWO MINUTES UNTIL
THE END OF THE UNIVERSE!

So what?

said Samuel Nathaniel Daniels.

The book started two and
a half years BEFORE
my tenth birthday.

Yes, I remember, said Bryan.

Bravo **wrecked** the rocket you had made, then lied to your mum, making her think it was **your fault.**

Right, said Compton.

The weird **thing** is that up until that day, he **hadn't** been mean to me <u>AT ALL</u>.

Compton looked at the others,

waiting for the penny to drop.

A mechanical voice **boomed** around the room:

ONE MINUTE UNTIL THE END OF THE UNIVERSE!

So you're suggesting,

said The Commissioner,

that we throw a **TIME BUBBLE** around the day when your brother turns into a bully?

Yeah, said Compton.

Yeah,

said Bryan, **finally** understanding the plan.

If we can stop that moment then he WON'T get nasty, which means that he WON'T steal the sandwich in the first place.

There's no guarantee of that,

said Samuel Nathaniel Daniels.

A mechanical voice **boomed** around the room:

THIRTY SECONDS UNTIL THE END OF THE UNIVERSE!

Do you have a better plan?

said Compton, looking first at Samuel Nathaniel Daniels and then at The Commissioner.

The Commissioner rubbed her chin.

Then:

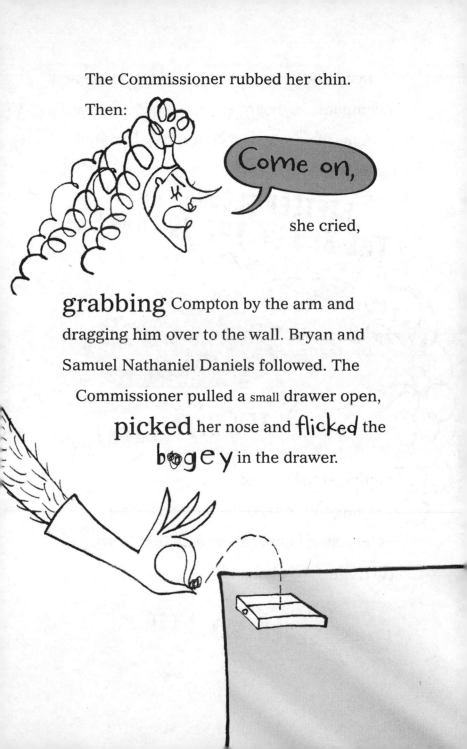

Come on,

she cried,

grabbing Compton by the arm and dragging him over to the wall. Bryan and Samuel Nathaniel Daniels followed. The Commissioner pulled a small drawer open, picked her nose and flicked the bogey in the drawer.

Instantly, three green lights flashed and a computer keyboard appeared out of the wall.

A mechanical voice boomed around the room:

FIFTEEN SECONDS UNTIL THE END OF THE UNIVERSE!

Quick, said The Commissioner. Put in the date and hit "ENTER".

TEN...NINE...EIGHT...

continued the countdown.

Compton pushed the buttons as fast as he could, inputting the date that Bravo wrecked his model rocket.

SEVEN...SIX...FIVE...

He hit "ENTER" and the words **TIME BUBBLE LOADING...** came up on the screen.

A moment later the air around them crackled and fizzed

and Compton, Bryan and Samuel Nathaniel Daniels

DISAPPEARED.

As they were sucked BACK IN TIME, they heard the last echoes of the mechanical voice booming around the room: "TWO - 'ONE -" echoes of the last echoes echoes

Chapter 28

Nearly Two-And-A-Half Years BEFORE Compton's Tenth Birthday

Next to a tree in a field just behind Morlock Cottage, Compton, Bryan and Samuel Nathaniel Daniels APPEARED from over six hundred years in the FUTURE.

"The TIME BUBBLE is holding," said Samuel Nathaniel Daniels, checking his W.A.T.CH. "But I don't know how long for."

"Come on," said Compton. "Let's get closer to the house and see what's going on.

Remember, we're looking for the moment that changed Bravo into a horrible bully."

The TIME-TRAVELLING TRIO carefully walked up to the hedge at the back of Morlock Cottage and peered into Compton's back garden. Through the kitchen window at the back of the house, Compton watched as the two-and-a-half year younger version of himself started to build a rocket, to enter at the village fête.

As he did so, the door of the garden shed *burst* open.

"Look!" cried Bryan. "It's Bravo. What's he doing?"

Sure enough, Bravo had emerged from the shed. He was carrying two large glass coffee jars and a cardboard box. One of the jars was full of frogspawn that Bravo had caught in the village pond, and in the other were hundreds of HAIRY caterpillars that he'd been collecting over the last few days. Bravo, who was extremely interested in wildlife and nature, was planning to WOW the village fête committee by recreating a village ecosystem in a cardboard box.

"What **on earth** is that *thing* on Bravo's **face?**" said Bryan.

"I *think* it's a **smile,**" said Samuel Nathaniel Daniels.

"**Unbelievable,**" said Bryan. "I don't think I've **ever** seen him **smile** before."*

Taking all the things he needed to build his ecosystem, Bravo went down the path to the front gate.

"What **on earth** is he doing with **his legs?**" said Bryan.

"Well, if I'm not mistaken, I *think* he's **skipping,**" said Samuel Nathaniel Daniels.

* Actually, this wasn't strictly true. Bryan had seen Bravo's face contort into a kind of hideous, evil smile whenever he was about to hit/hurt/yell at/scare someone. What he meant was that he had never seen Bravo smile without also seeing someone cry about three seconds later.

Bryan let out a long whistle.

"INCREDIBLE," he said, shaking his head. "Simply incredible."

As they continued to watch Bravo smiling and skipping, he did something odd. He was just about to go out of the front gate and cross the road when he swerved and ducked down quickly behind a bush.

What's he doing? whispered Bryan.

Dunno, said Compton.

It looks like he's hiding.

Look, someone's coming.

said Samuel Nathaniel Daniels.

Compton and Bryan turned their heads and looked to where Samuel Nathaniel Daniels was pointing. Coming up the road towards Morlock Cottage was a girl wearing a brilliant white dress and carrying a plate with an ENORMOUS chocolate cake on it.

That's Nancy,

said Compton.

I remember her. She lived down the road for a bit. Her family moved away a couple of years ago.

They watched as Nancy came nearer and nearer.

Compton's voice trailed off as he struggled to claw back the memory from the depths of his brain. But his attempts were sidetracked by what happened next. Something even odder was happening to Bravo. As he hid behind the bush, he started VIOLENTLY SHAKING his head.

"What's he doing?" whispered Samuel Nathaniel Daniels.

"Dunno," said Compton. "It looks like he's going mad."

As they continued to watch, they realized why Bravo was shaking his head. When he'd ducked down behind the bush he had disturbed a wasp that was also in the bush. *

* Quite by chance the wasp was also hiding from someone – a rather pretty lady wasp that was across the road.

Taking the greatest of exceptions to being disturbed, the wasp had begun a sustained, triple-play attack on Bravo. Not wanting to let go of his precious jars, he was trying to deter the wasp using VIGOROUS SHAKES of his head. The plan was not going well however, as the headshakes only seemed to make the wasp more determined to sting Bravo.

As Nancy came closer and closer, the wasp attack reached its dramatic conclusion with the wasp administering a first-class sting to Bravo's bottom. What happened next seemed to take place in slow motion. After receiving the painful bottom sting, Bravo fell forward in SHOCK.

He tumbled through the bush and onto the pavement. As he did so, the jars containing the frogspawn and caterpillars flew HIGH up into the air. As they shot skywards, the lids came off and the frogspawn and caterpillars flew free.

As terrible luck would have it, just as Bravo was stung, Nancy Flowers was walking past. Out of the corner of her eye she saw the blur of Bravo falling through the bush. Then, as she turned her head to see what was happening, some frogspawn hit her straight in the face, going into her mouth and up her nose.

As she reeled from this, she was horrified to find a **shower of caterpillars** raining down on her head. The **caterpillars** went **EVERYWHERE** – in her ears, in her hair, down her dress and into the cake.

And then, just when Nancy thought this minute **couldn't** get

ANY WORSE,

she stepped onto some

frogspawn

that had

fallen on the

ground and

SKIDDED.

As she fell backwards, she let go of her ENORMOUS chocolate cake, which also flew

HIGH up into the air.

Nancy landed **painfully** on her bottom with a **BUMP** – and a split second later, the chocolate cake **smashed down** on top of her **beautiful, new** and **brilliant** white dress.

Compton, Bryan and Samuel Nathaniel Daniels stood open-mouthed at what they had just seen.

Bravo **staggered** to his feet and rushed over to help poor Nancy Flowers up.

"Nancy!" he cried. "I-I-I—"

But before he could say anything else, a **GIGANTIC,** *high-pitched,* ear-popping SHRIEK came out of Nancy's mouth.

BRAVO VALANCE! she yelled. I HATE YOU!

And with that, she burst into tears and ran home.

Bravo didn't know what to do. He had accidentally ruined the dress, cake and day of the girl who he loved from afar. He felt terrible, but at the same time, he also felt that it hadn't really been his fault. It was the wasp – the stupid, sting-y wasp.

At the *very moment* that all these
thoughts and feelings were *swirling*
around his brain,

a car passed by. The car's windows were
wide open and through them Bravo could hear
some strange music. As he looked at the mess
of cake and frogspawn and caterpillars
on the ground, the wailing chorus
of ULTRA WARRIOR SCUM'S
debut song, "You're UGLY
Like a Poodle's Bum",
blared out across the street and into his ears.

"Oh my," said Samuel Nathaniel Daniels. "That was unfortunate. He really liked her, did he?"

"Yes," said Compton, feeling a bit sorry for his brother. "He *really* did."

"Well," said Samuel Nathaniel Daniels, checking his W.A.T.CH., "it says here that Nancy and her family moved away not long after because her dad got a job in another town. This was the last time Bravo ever saw Nancy."

"Then that must have been the moment we were looking for," said Compton.

Wait, said Bryan.

Something else is happening. LOOK.

They watched as the WORST BULLY in Little Hadron joined Bravo on the pavement, a boy called Vinnie Skinster. He was fifteen and had terrorized the neighbourhood for the previous two years. He had also seen everything that had just happened.

CLASSIC! he said, clapping Bravo on the back.

Absolutely classic. You must have been planning THAT for ages. That was easily the BEST PRANK I have ever seen. Did you see her face when she got up? BRILLIANT, JUST BRILLIANT.

I don't, er, I mean, I didn't...

said Bravo, struggling to get his words out.

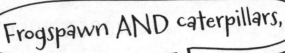

Frogspawn AND caterpillars, continued Skinster.

Now, **THAT** was a touch of **GENIUS**.

This was **INCREDIBLE**. Bravo had **never** dared to even look Vinnie Skinster in the eye before, but here he was, laughing at something Bravo had done. A peculiar swell of happiness grew in Bravo's chest and he let out a snigger.

Yeah, it was quite funny, wasn't it?

he said.

Quite? QUITE? It was BRILLIANT, said Skinster.

You wanna come down to the village fête later on and stick your fingers into cakes and throw vegetables on the floor?

Bravo felt an excitement building inside him that he had never experienced before.

"Yeah," he said. "Great. Meet you down there in half an hour."

And with that, Compton, Bryan and Samuel Nathaniel Daniels watched as Bravo walked back through the front gate of Morlock Cottage and into the kitchen, where he took the model rocket that seven-and-a-half-year-old Compton had made, threw it on the floor and started jumping UP and DOWN on it.

Behind the hedge outside Morlock Cottage,
Compton *whispered* his plan to the others.
Samuel Nathaniel Daniels nodded his head,
pushed some buttons on his **W.A.T.CH.**
and, as the air around them
crackled and fizzed, they all

DISAPPEARED.

Chapter 29

Nearly Two And A Half Years BEFORE Compton's Tenth Birthday (Again)

Next to the tree, in a field just behind Morlock Cottage, Compton, Bryan and Samuel Nathaniel Daniels appeared from over six hundred years in the FUTURE.

"The TIME BUBBLE is holding," said Samuel Nathaniel Daniels checking his W.A.T.CH. "But I don't know how long for."

"Come on," said Compton. "Let's get closer to the house and see what's going on.

Remember, we're looking for the moment that changed Bravo into a **horrible bully**."

The **TIME-TRAVELLING TRIO** carefully walked up to the hedge at the back of Morlock Cottage and **peered** into Compton's back garden. Through the kitchen window at the back of the house, Compton watched as the **two-and-a-half year younger** version of himself started to build a **rocket,** to enter at the village fête.

As he did so, the door of the garden shed *burst* open.

"Look!" cried Bryan. "It's Bravo. What's he doing?"

Sure enough, Bravo had emerged from the shed. He was carrying two large glass coffee jars and a cardboard box. One of the jars was full of frogspawn that Bravo had caught in the village pond, and in the other were hundreds of HAIRY caterpillars that he'd been collecting over the last few days. Bravo, who was extremely interested in wildlife and nature, was planning to WOW the village fête committee by recreating a village ecosystem in a cardboard box.

"What on earth is that thing on Bravo's face?" said Bryan.

"I think it's a smile," said Samuel Nathaniel Daniels.

"Unbelievable," said Bryan. "I don't think I've ever seen him smile before."

As they were talking, Compton noticed the air beside them start to crackle and fizz. "What's that?"

Before anyone could answer, the strangest thing happened. As if out of nowhere, another Compton, Bryan and Samuel Nathaniel Daniels

APPEARED

"That's WEIRD," said Bryan, in what could well have been a contender for UNDERSTATEMENT OF THE YEAR.*

Compton looked at Compton, who looked at Bryan, who was looking at Bryan looking at Samuel Nathaniel Daniels. He was looking at his W.A.T.CH.

* That year the winning entry in the UNDERSTATEMENT OF THE YEAR AWARDS went to Albarious Heritage from Doncaster who, after seeing a lady suck a whole pint of milk up through her nose and then cry it out of her eyes, sniffed and said, "That's quite odd, isn't it?".

The Compton who had just arrived
tapped the side of his nose.

"Don't worry," he said. "We'll sort
this out."

Then he and the Bryan who had just
arrived and the Samuel Nathaniel
Daniels who had just arrived went into
a huddle and whispered to each other.

The first Samuel
Nathaniel Daniels
tapped some buttons
on his W.A.T.CH.

"I think they're from a few
minutes in the future," he said.
"They must have seen the moment
that Bravo turns into a MEAN BULLY
and know how to fix it."

Sure enough, the Compton, Bryan
and Samuel Nathaniel Daniels
from a few minutes in the future

waited until Bravo hid behind the bush,
then they sprang into action. As they did,
the other Compton noticed that the sky
appeared to be darkening.

What's THAT?

he said.

Samuel Nathaniel Daniels tapped
some more on his **W.A.T.CH.**

It's the TIME BUBBLE,

he said.

It's running out of energy
and will COLLAPSE at
any minute. That darkness
is the END OF THE
UNIVERSE.
That lot had better
know what
they're doing.

Over behind the bush, Bravo crouched down and hid from Nancy Flowers. He **really, *really*** liked her but was so shy that he didn't know what to say. Suddenly he felt a buzzing in his ears and caught sight of a BIG, **fat**, ANGRY wasp launching an attack. Bravo screwed his eyes TIGHTLY SHUT and shook his head FURIOUSLY. As he did so, Compton-from-a-few-minutes-in-the-future crept up, *swished* his

arm around

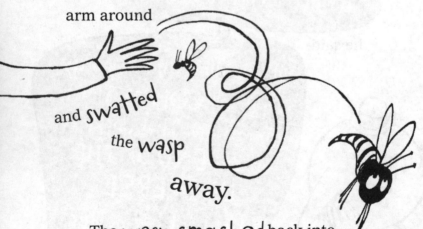

and swatted the wasp away.

The wasp smashed back into the bush, was momentarily stunned and then woozily buzzed off.

Once the **wasp** had gone, Compton-from-a-few-minutes-in-the-future rejoined Bryan-from-a-few-minutes-in-the-future, who was hiding behind a tree.

After a moment, Bravo realized that the **buzzing** had stopped and opened his eyes. When he did, he saw that Nancy had been joined by a **strange man** wearing a **tight** silver suit.

"*Hello,*" the man said to her. "Are you on your way to the fête?"

"**Yes,**" said Nancy, a little wary of the **oddly** dressed stranger.

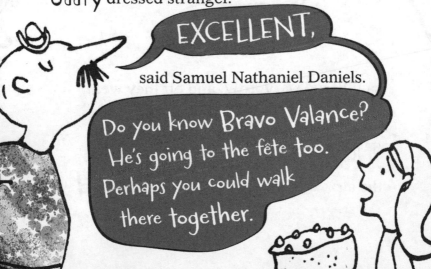

EXCELLENT,

said Samuel Nathaniel Daniels.

Do you know Bravo Valance? He's going to the fête too. Perhaps you could walk there together.

And with that, Samuel Nathaniel Daniels reached into the bush, grabbed Bravo and **pulled him out.**

Oh, er, yes that'd be lovely,

said Nancy, a little shocked.

Hi, Bravo. Fancy coming to the fête?

Okay,

said Bravo nervously, and off they went.

One second later, just as the

TIME BUBBLE COLLAPSED,

the air crackled and fizzed

and Compton, Compton-from-a-few-minutes-in-the-future, Bryan, Bryan-from-a few-minutes-in-the-future, Samuel Nathaniel Daniels and Samuel-Nathaniel-Daniels-from-a few-minutes-in-the-future ALL DISAPPEARED.

Chapter 30

Goodbye

COMPTON! shouted Mr Valance from downstairs.

Stop THUMPING AROUND and get a move on. EVERYONE'S WAITING.*

"COMING, DAD," shouted Compton, before turning to Samuel Nathaniel Daniels. "So what happens *NOW*?"

Samuel Nathaniel Daniels opened the wardrobe in Compton's bedroom and pulled out a shoebox.

"Well, thanks to you, Bravo never did get his hands on the TIME MACHINE,

---

* In case you were wondering, we are now right back where we started.

302

THE UNIVERSE is safe for another hundred trillion years or so, and now I need to return to FPU headquarters and destroy this sandwich."

He opened the shoebox and immediately wished he hadn't. The smell of a thousand unwashed armpits, combined with the odour of a hundred rotten eggs, mingled with the reek of a trainer that someone with athlete's foot has worn without socks for eight weeks straight, blended with the tang of six hundred stinky, soiled nappies, all smashed up Samuel Nathaniel Daniels's nostrils like an elephant wearing jet-powered rocket boots.

Samuel Nathaniel Daniels tried to avert his nose but it was **too late** and the **whiff** melted all the hairs on the inside of his **nasal cavity.***

Blimey, said Compton, holding his nose.

I think you're **right.** I think I'll **stick** with this **TIMELINE** for a bit.

Would have been **nice** to have **fought** Blackbeard though, said Bryan sadly.

* This wasn't such a bad thing as Samuel Nathaniel Daniels was well known in **FPU** circles for having the longest nose hairs of **ALL** the agents. He'd been growing one for years and had named it **Gertie.**

"Sorry, guys," said Samuel Nathaniel Daniels. "But The Commissioner has INSISTED. I don't want to mess up again."

"Something has been bothering me," said Compton. "Couldn't we have just gone back to before Bravo first stole the sandwich and stopped him stealing the sandwich?"

"Yeah," said Bryan. "Then THE UNIVERSE wouldn't have been in danger."

Well, actually, said Samuel Nathaniel Daniels, THAT would have triggered TIMELINE 12,345, which would have led to the DESTRUCTION OF THE UNIVERSE in THREE WEEKS.

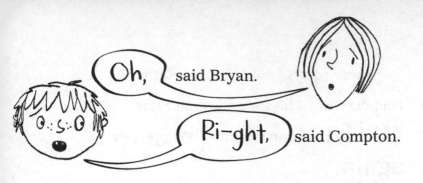

"Oh," said Bryan.

"Ri-ght," said Compton.

Then he clapped Bryan on the shoulder. "Come on, let's go and get some pizza."

As they were leaving the room, Compton turned to Samuel Nathaniel Daniels.

"Thanks for EVERYTHING, Samuel," he said.

"It really has been the BEST TWO DAYS of my life."

"Mine too," said Bryan. "Especially the whole 'saving the universe' thing. That was really cool."

306

"Gentlemen," said Samuel Nathaniel Daniels, pushing some buttons on his **W.A.T.CH.**, "it has been an honour." And with that, the air in Compton's bedroom crackled and fizzed and Samuel Nathaniel Daniels DISAPPEARED.

After a moment, Compton and Bryan went downstairs to join the others.

"What were you doing up there?" asked Compton's dad.

Compton smiled at Bryan.

"You know, nothing much," he replied. "Stopping THE UNIVERSE from being destroyed by Bravo, that kind of thing."

Mr Valance looked at Compton for a moment, then burst into laughter.

HA HA HA, HA HA HA HA...

"Yeah, right," he said, ruffling Compton's hair. "Come on, let's have some fun."

Chapter 31

The Future Perfect Unit's Perfect Future

651 years after Compton Valance first realized he had created a **TIME MACHINE**, a **man in a black suit** was talking to The Commissioner in a super-secret office, which no one knew was there because it was hidden behind a door marked:

• WOMEN'S TOILETS

OUT OF ORDER

"So everything is back to normal?" said the man in the black suit, rubbing his fingers along a strange scar on his face.

The Commissioner was sitting behind her desk. She stroked her chin gently.

Yes, thanks to Compton Valance. His plan worked a treat. They managed to alter the future by changing Bravo's timeline. He is no longer a bully, so he DIDN'T eavesdrop on his brother talking about the sandwich, DIDN'T know of its existence and so DIDN'T steal it and cause the DESTRUCTION OF THE UNIVERSE.

COMMISSIONER

Excellent, said the man.

So where's the sandwich now?

"The sandwich
has been retrieved,"
said The Commissioner.
"Agent Daniels has assured me
that he will prepare his report by
tomorrow morning."

"Is there anything else I can do?"
said the man in the black suit.

"Yes, Susan, there is,"
said The Commissioner.*
"There were a few other
changes that happened as
a result of Compton changing
his brother's TIMELINE.
They will need to be corrected."

* In the year 2367, the name Susan gets changed
from a girl's name to a boy's name. The same happens
in reverse for Peter.

Susan nodded his head and turned to go. As he did, he caught sight of a document on The Commissioner's screen. The document was marked with the words:

TOP SECRET – COMPTON VALANCE: TIME CRIME AGENT (IN TRAINING).

What's THAT? he asked.

It's the FUTURE, said The Commissioner.

I have a proposal for you, Susan. Compton Valance could become a VERY important asset to the Future Perfect Unit. VERY IMPORTANT INDEED.

Chapter 32

Epilogue

Samuel Nathaniel Daniels *raced* around his office in a state of high PANIC. He was *supposed* to be arranging for the disposal of Compton's TIME MACHINE SANDWICH but he had completely FORGOTTEN what he'd done with it.

The intercom unit buzzed on his desk.

AGENT DANIELS,

barked The Commissioner's voice.

Have you DISPOSED of the sandwich yet?

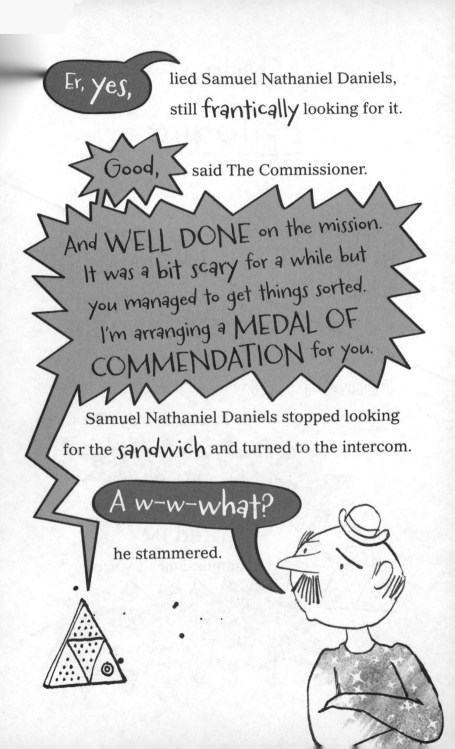

Since the baked bean incident,
The Commissioner had shouted at him
at every opportunity and now here she
was telling him he was going to get a medal.

You helped save
THE UNIVERSE,

said The Commissioner.

You deserve it. The ceremony will
take place in the boardroom on the
tenth floor in five minutes.
Over and out.

The intercom switched off.

FIVE MINUTES?

yelled Samuel Nathaniel Daniels.
And he started looking for his smart
silver suit that had tassles down the side
and his new bowler hat.

An hour later, Samuel Nathaniel Daniels CMW* was standing in his smartest outfit with a *huge* GOLD MEDAL pinned to his chest.

Ah, Daniels,

said The Commissioner, coming over to him.

I hope you're coming to the party? It's not every day you stop the DESTRUCTION OF THE UNIVERSE. You haven't got ANYTHING else to do, have you? I'm sure the paperwork can wait until tomorrow.

* Commendation Medal Winner

Samuel Nathaniel Daniels remembered that he **hadn't** disposed of Compton's TIME MACHINE SANDWICH yet.

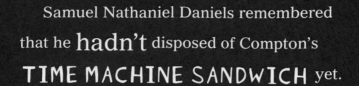

Ah well, he thought to himself.

The sandwich *can wait. I mean, I* **know** *it nearly* **destroyed** THE UNIVERSE *and it was* only *thanks to Compton and Bryan's quick thinking that we all survived, but, really, that's* **not** *going to happen again,* is it?

And with **that,** he went to the **party.**

Travel BACK IN TIME to Compton and Bryan's FIRST eye-wateringly EXCELLENT adventure, where the boys discover that Compton's mouldy old SANDWICH has turned into a TIME MACHINE and they are now the MOST POWERFUL BOYS in THE UNIVERSE...

"Funny, clever, brilliant – I love this book. Buy it immediately!" Dermot O'Leary

COMPTON VALANCE

The Most POWERFUL BOY in the UNIVERSE

BY MATT BROWN

And, whizz six hundred years into the **FUTURE** to join **Compton** and **Bryan** on their **THIRD** brain-meltingly **BRILLIANT** escapade, as the boys become **TIME CRIME AGENTS IN TRAINING** and set out to save the world from

TOTAL DESTRUCTION

once more...

COMPTON VALANCE 3

COMING 2015

Zoom over to

www.comptonvalance.com

for loads more SANDWICHES, TIME-TRAVELLING MAYHEM and SUPER-TOP-SECRET STUFF!

Acknowledgements

To the Barry girls –
Mum, Sam and Megs

One of the things I've learned while writing this book
is that every author needs A LOT of help along the way
and so here I would like to say a big THANK YOU
to a few people who have lent a hand.

Firstly, I need to thank Lizzie Finlay for her insanely
awesome illustrations. Thanks as well to Dr Iain Morley
from the University of Oxford. I had a wonderful chat with him
one afternoon when he tried to cram everything he knows about
Homo Heidelbergensis into my brain (and he knows a LOT!).
Big thanks to all the BROWNS and CLARES who were
brilliant and helped find ways to let me write the book
at all hours of the day and night (especially Joe, who was my
first reader and joke tester). Thanks to everyone at Usborne
who have been so helpful, funny, clever and brilliant but
especially Amy Dobson and Anna Howorth for their amazingly
inventive ideas (and great car chats), Rebecca Hill for making
me write two books, Becky Walker for her infinite enthusiasm,
kindness, encouragement and skill, and Hannah Cobley
and all the design team who make the Compton books
look so SUPERCOOL. Thanks too to the Heart posse,
especially Gareth, Babs and Ross for all their support.

Finally, thank you to YOU if you have read the book,
bought the book, borrowed the book, recommended the book,
reviewed the book, tweeted about the book, sold the book,
gifted the book, had the book on your shelf to impress your
friends, or have just this second opened the back page of
the book in the bookshop to see if the ending is any good.
THANK YOU, THANK YOU, THANK YOU!